The Bellus Curse

Leon Michaels

Acknowledgement

To my Wife and Proof Reader who told me the original version of this tale stunk to high heaven, and not to publish it.

She was right and 14 hours of editing, rewrite and the addition of over 1400 words fixed the problem.

I hope!

Books By Leon Michaels

The Path Home

From the Mists of Darkness

Task Force Nemesis

Tales From The Bench

The Echelon Factor

The Morbius Expedition

Three Against The Darkness

Random Acts Of Science Fiction

Willem

Today is Yesterday's Tomorrow

A Rigged Deck

"The Denoyelles Family Saga"

The Hanover Throne

The Bellus Project

The Bellus Legacy

The Bellus Myth

The Bellus Solution

The Bellus Prophecy

The Phoenix Project

"The Crane Equation Trilogy"

The Crane Equation: The Early Years

The Crane Equation: Rebuilding a Nation

The Crane Equation: The Crane Legacy

"The Black Ops Series"

Operation Damocles

Operation Dokkaebi

Operation Yofune-Nushi

Operation Kartikeya

The Black Orchid

The Twenty-First Special Operations Group: Book One: Family

The Twenty-First Special Operations Group: Book Two: Operators

Operation Heracles

Operation Pandora

This is a work of Fiction. Any similarities to individuals past or present is unintentional and purely a coincidence. Any similarities to any individual in the future is pure Karma.

This Page Left Blank

A New World

The pilot was in his eighth orbit of a Class M Planet as he watched the sensor data scrolling on his cockpit monitor. He had yet to find any indication of human life on the planet, or even the remains of a once population on this world. The world was unmarred by the remains of settlements or towns.

The planet was about sixty percent water with three continents laid out almost an equal distance apart. Each continent showed animal life, with the largest continent having large herds of animals moving across its plains. Sensor readings gave indications. one herd contained nearly ten thousand large animals, standing approximately three meters tall and as long as five meters.

He took one last look at the external sensor readings to ensure he was alone over the planet before leaving the cockpit to fix something to eat, as he decided to make two more orbits before landing to collect mineral samples. The sensors had already told him this was a rich world, but he needed the samples to confirm the quality of its assets.

Before he could even get out of the cockpit, he heard the distinctive pinging sound of his communications crystal which his parents had installed in his comm unit. The Hayutan Communications Crystal was a unique piece of technology as it allowed instantaneous communications between two or more parties anywhere in the universe.

Hayutan Communications Crystals were restricted to specific Fleet vessels or members of the Royal family. This vessel was no longer a Fleet vessel and it was registered to one Carlos Henreid of New Brumsfield. The vessel was once an Atlas Class Scout Ship that had been completely stripped then rebuilt at the Hayutan Shipyards for the single purpose of one Earl Carlos Gannaway, son of Baron Lucen Gannaway, for his personal use.

And its use was for prospecting beyond the boundaries of the known universe.

Carlos had joined the Fleet as a Construction Engineer after getting his university degree in Geology. After he completed his enlistment in the Hayutan Fleet, he told his father that he was going out to make his own name in the universe, and with luck, his own fortune as a prospector. His father had the Scout Ship rebuilt and registered under Carlos' mother's maiden name on her home planet.

Ducking back into the cockpit, Carlos activated the communications crystal. His mother was at the other end of the connection.

"Yes mother?"

"Carlos, you are twenty-four hours late checking in."

Carlos had agreed to check in with his parents once a week while out surveying planets for mining and had indeed missed his weekly report.

"Sorry mother, I'm in orbit over what looks like a very rich world. I plan on filing a claim on the planet within the hour and I just got caught up in reading the sensor data."

She smiled at him.

"Carlos, you have always been easily distracted. But we have good news, your sister Selina is expecting."

"That's great mother. I doubt that I'll be back in time for the birth, so will you get a gift for me?"

"I shall. Now I know you are busy, so please be safe and we'll talk again at your next check-in."

"Love you mother and give father my love. Tell the brat I'm excited about her pregnancy and still amazed she found a man who can tolerate her."

"Carlos, I'll just give her your love because I will not be your hatchet man, even if you are just joking."

Carlos laughed as he watched his mother disconnect the link. He had fought the idea of reporting in weekly, but he had to admit that the reports were a nice break from being out alone in the universe.

After a quick meal, Carlos organized the sensor data into a report of this world. Attached the navigational data to it. Then after double checking the Federation Application for claiming the planet, he submitted it not only to the Federation Planetary Foundation, but a copy to his Aunt, his Father's Sister who had just ascended the Throne when his Grandfather had retired.

With the notation on his application of a copy to the Throne, he knew that the Planetary Foundation would process his claim immediately and only disapprove it if the paperwork was not properly filled out.

Once his system showed the paperwork had been transmitted, he did the calculations to make planetfall on the largest continent.

Riches & Natives

The first place Carlos landed was in a small valley high up in the Southern mountains below the snow line. Senor readings showed this area was heavy with a crystalline formation similar to those used to make the Hayutan Communication Crystals. His first clue was the vein of platinum running through an outcropping of rock. When he found the vein of crystal, he could only smile as it was nearly ninety-eight percent pure. This alone made him richer than his family trust fund could provide.

Carlos set down in five different locations over the first week, taking samples and testing them in his compact lab aboard his ship, then sending those results back to the Federation utilizing his own communications crystal to speed up the process, and by directing them through his family, no one in the Federation would dare misplace the reports and filings.

His ancestors had changed much of the claims process for prospectors as a measure of preventing a single family as his from becoming too wealthy, too powerful by claiming a planet such has the discoverer of the Hanover System. The Denoyelles Family's wealth was now based upon industry. Business, not the riches ripped from the soil of a planet.

Because of this, Carlos could expect at best a thirty percent share of the mineral wealth of this planet, and no worse than twenty percent. Even at twenty percent, his wealth could exceed the wealth of the last Count of Hanover, Count Conrad by several billion Crowns, then add in the percentage of land fees, settler fees the Federation would share with him just added to the pot.

Not every planet discovered by prospectors, or explorers was this rich and usually those people were financed by a consortium, partners which sliced the wealth into smaller shares, but he financed his own venture from his trust fund and he would gain every percentage once the planet was exploited.

At his fourth test site, he confirmed the one item that would insure his wealth and that was a large vein of Iridium which was normally mined from asteroids in limited quantities. He processed the test results and transmitted them before moving to the next spot.

The fifth spot was in a heavily forested area and he considered himself lucky that he was able to sit down in a small clearing well inside the region. His test site was just meters inside the tree line and there was very little underbrush in the area to inhibit his movement.

His sensors showed a few animals in the area, with several of them as large as he was, so as he set up his equipment, he kept his head on a swivel, checking to insure nothing came up on him even though his sensors were linked to his helmet.

Carlos received a warning of an approaching creature from his left, but the sensor did not clarify manner, animal or human. He let the equipment continue its depth survey as he turned to look for anything which might harm him. What he saw moving through the forest took him by surprise.

At approximately one hundred meters away was what looked like a person walking towards him, but not just any person, a Centaurian. He amplified his helmets vision and what was coming towards him appeared to be a female Centaurian, with a long mane of Golden hair with ribbons in it.

She was dressed for combat in a black halter and panties but was not wearing boots as she appeared to be bare footed. It also appeared she had straps all around her body and legs until he amplified again and realized the darkness he was seeing was the color of her fur. She was stripped like a Liger, and the ribbons in her hair was the same dark color.

Her face was covered in fur but appeared to be almost human in form except the eyes. The eyes were larger than human norm and were yellow, much like a domestic cat. There was a long blade hanging from her left hip and in her right hand appeared to be a walking staff as tall as she was. He could hardly take his eyes off this creature as her movements were almost sexual with each step she took.

But the thing that truly set her apart from any Centaurian he had known was that she had a tail. A tail such as the felines of his own world were born with trailing behind her.

She was about thirty meters away when she quickly shifted the walking staff, taking it in both hands and pointing the end at him. Before he could raise his hands in peace or speak, it seemed to him a fire jumped from the end of the staff, enveloping his body, sending his nerve endings into overdrive and he passed out from the effect.

The female walked to his crumpled body and looked down at him, then kneeled down and carefully removed his helmet to get a better look at him. She brushed his beard with her hand before standing up and moving to the test equipment. It only took her a moment to determine the power button and turned off the equipment.

Making New Friends?

Carlos woke to find himself in a very compromising position. He was hanging from a tree limb with his feet touching the ground, arms extended above his head. And he was completely naked.

As his vision cleared he could see the female squatting a few meters in front of him with all of his clothing and gear spread out on the ground, examining it. His small pack had been opened with the mylar rain shield laid out and the small items from the pack and his pockets were neatly laid out on it.

His head was pounding as he watched her finger the things on the rain shield with her long fingers gently touching each item, moving it a millimeter then moving to the next item. As uncomfortable as he was and with his head aching, he tried not to make any noise as he watched her, trying to determine just how bad his situation was. He must have groaned as she looked up at him, slightly tilting her head to the right.

"You are awake human. Good."

She had a slight lisp in her speech and she spoke the word human in two parts, saying hu-man. As she stood, her tail, which had been up over her shoulder, stretched out, then wrapped itself around her waist.

"What are you called human?"

"Carlos. My name is Carlos. Yours?"

"I am Marta. I am the warder for this world. What is your purpose here?"

"I am a prospector."

"I do not know this word, prospector."

"I search for metals, minerals, riches to ease my way in life."

"Have you found such riches here?"

"Yes Marta, I have. Riches beyond my dreams."

"Carlos, I know your language, but not all of its meanings. Tell me what riches you have found and how you will receive them."

"There are metals, minerals under the soil that my race needs as we travel through space. Other humans will come, settle this world, farm the land and others were dig into the soil to remove those minerals. How do you know my language?"

"My people have listened to your voices long before I was born. We have met your people before as they traveled into this region of space. But this is a protected world, your people cannot come here. To do so would destroy all that we protect. I cannot allow you to tell your humans about this world."

"Then we have a problem Marta, as they already know."

She walked up close to him and her tail gently slide down his body. He shivered from its fine fur touching his bare skin.

"That is not good human. Many will die if they come here. Your race and mine, and the balance of nature here will be destroyed."

Her tail continued to move over his body then she raised her hand to his chest, gently touching it, then she pulled it back, so he could see her hand and suddenly claws extended from her fingertips. She raked her claws down his chest, barely scratching his skin before stepping back from him.

"You interest me human, too bad you must die."

"Wait Marta! My race has laws, rules to prevent this world from being settled. But I must contact my people to let them know about your race and this world being protected."

"As I have spoken, my people have met your race before and those we met were vile creatures. They even mistreated their own race."

"Slavers. Those were probably slavers that were driven deep into space away from mine. Let me speak to my people, my family and I can stop my people from coming here."

She looked at him with her golden eyes seeming to dig deep into his soul.

"How can I trust you human?"

"You cannot. Not with the history your people have with mine if I understand you correctly. But the trust between races has to start somewhere. Is this not a good place to start?"

She raised her clawed hand up to his face once more.

"Human, Carlos, I swore an oath to protect this world and the creatures which are upon it. If you deceive me, with my last breath I will tear the flesh from your bones and feed it to the Kamora."

"I accept your oath to kill me as truth Marta. But I have to go to my ship to contact my people."

"Carlos, I will release you, but you can only cover your manhood. Nothing else which might harm me."

"I agree to your terms Marta."

She pulled her long knife from its sheath, then reached over his head and sliced through the vine she had tied him up with, then quickly stepped back from him. She then held her knife out, edge up and he cut through the vines that had his hands tied together and worked his fingers to get the blood flowing back into them.

Marta moved away, picking up her staff as she did so, allowing Carlos to move to his things. He picked up his briefs, shook them a couple times to shake off any leaves or insects that may have gotten on them before putting them on.

"Marta, I have a headache from what you did to me with your staff. I'm going to get a pain reliever and water."

She just nodded as she pointed her staff at him. Carlos kneeled down and picked up a small bottle from his things, opened it and shook two pills out onto the palm of his hand, showing them to her before putting the cap back on the bottle. He then carefully reached over to his canteen, picked it up and then popped the pills into his mouth before opening the canteen and taking a long drink. Once he had accomplished that, he resealed the canteen and just dropped it back onto the ground before standing up.

Carlos put his hands on top of his head and began walking to his ship. He had to watch each step as he was barefooted and not accustomed to walking in such a manner. At the access panel of his ship he turned so she could see what he was doing and left one hand on his head as he punched in the access code to open the hatch.

He made sure the hatch was fully open before stepping through it with his hands still on his head and trying to make sure she could see him clearly as he slowly moved through the ship to the command console. Carlos stopped short of the command chair and slowly turned to her.

"Marta, I have to sit down so I can activate my communications systems. Relax, there is nothing in here to harm you."

She only nodded as she held her staff at the ready to give him another shot of whatever it was that knocked him out. He carefully took the command chair and with only one hand, activated the communications crystal to his parents. He had no idea of the time on Hayuta, but he hoped someone would answer his call. Moments later his mother's image appeared. She looked at Carlos with his hands on his head and as far as she could tell, naked before her. She carefully leaned forward and pressed a button on the console she was sitting at.

Marta felt the electric charge emanating from the metal floor panels up through body and she froze, then collapsed from the shock. Carlos's mother released the button before speaking.

"Carlos, what was that behind you?"

"Mother, it appears I have not only discovered a very rich planet, I have discovered a new race. Let me deal with the individual you just shocked then I will get right back to you, but advise the Throne to quarantine this world under the Articles concerning the discovery of a new, alien race."

"Alright Carlos be careful and get back to me as quickly as possible."

"I will mother."

He moved back to where Marta had fallen and looked at her a moment before picking her up from the deck. She was heavier than she looked, and he just placed her on his bunk, then placed her staff next to her. For a brief moment he was tempted to do to her what she had done to him, strip her of her garments, but he knew that to build a dialogue, trust between them he could not do that.

Looking at her, he felt is she was devoid of the fur, and tail she would look as human as any female he had met. Granted her eyes were larger, more almond shaped and of course the gold color instead of the milky white of a normal human. And her lips were fuller, thicker than norm, but still attractive under her pug like nose.

No, without a doubt, she was a feline, but one unlike the human race had ever seen before.

He quickly dressed as he watched her unsure when she would awake. Carlos figured if things worked out, he could collect his things left at the test site later. This time he did not strap on his spare pistol but did attach his Wakizashi, his short sword to his hip since he knew there was no way he could defend himself against her claws if she attacked him except for the sword.

Carlos considered checking her with his pocket Doc, but without a base line for her species, he knew that it would not do any good. He sipped on fruit juice as he watched her slowly arouse from the shock which slammed her to the deck.

She slowly woke up then jerked upright, looking around the cabin of his ship. Her hand went to her long knife at her hip, but Carlos had already unsheathed his short sword and was slapping it on his leg to let her know he was now armed.

"Marta are you ready to talk about peace between your people and mine?"

"There can be no peace if your race comes to destroy this world."

"Marta, I have already sent word back to my people to stop such a thing from happening. We have laws to prevent such things. The people who your race has met before did not concern themselves with laws, only greed. Notice, you have your weapons and are not exposed to me as I was to you. If I meant you harm, it would have already been done."

"What did you do to me to put me at your mercy?"

"That I shall not tell you until I am certain that we can talk freely as friends, not as adversaries."

"What is adversaries?"

"Enemies."

"How can I be sure that your people will not come here and destroy this world searching for riches?"

"Leave your staff on the bed, and we shall talk to my parents. It was my mother you saw before you were knocked out. Talk to her and my father. They will tell you what I have told you about our laws."

"How do I know you will not subdue me again?"

"You sit in the chair. It will prevent you from being harmed."

Her eyes narrowed and if she had feline ears he was certain they would be laid back, ready for a fight. After a few moments, her features softened.

"Yes, I will sit in your chair and talk to your elders."

Carlos stood, flipped his sword and guided it back into his sheath. Her eyes widened at his display in handling the sword. Slowly she moved from his bunk and he motioned for her to go ahead of him, so she could take his chair. His cockpit had a second, pull-out chair, but he did not retrieve it, he just waited until she was seated then he reached passed her and activated the crystal.

Both of his parents were in view this time. His father spoke first.

"Carlos, what is your status?"

"Neutral at this time Father. May I introduce Marta who I hope will accept our truth concerning this world and become a friend to the human race. But I must advise you that her people have had contact with slavers and are not pleased with that contact."

His father sat for a moment in thought before speaking.

19

"Marta, I am Baron Lucen Gannaway, Carlos's father and this is his mother, Baroness Patrina Gannaway."

"Pardon my not understanding. I do not know this Baron or Baroness."

"Marta, it is only a title. A word used to show our position in our society. Carlos can explain it all to you later but right now there is something we need to ask of you. We need you to do something which will not harm you, but will help us as we help Carlos protect your world."

"Carlos said he came here to discover riches. Why would you deny him his riches?"

Lucen smiled at her question.

"Marta, it is the burden of our family to protect those who would be harmed by humanity. Carlos said that your people have had contact with those we call slavers. Our family drove those people deep into space, away from the rest of humanity because of their evil intent. You are a new race, a new species which we are bound by honor and law to protect from harm. You can see the scars on my face which are the result from a battle to protect those who are not able to protect themselves from evil."

"You are warriors?"

"Yes, in many ways we are warriors. Even Carlos's mother studied to be a warrior to protect her people before we married."

"What is married?"

"Mated, bonded to one another for life."

"There is much to learn about your people Baron. What do you require of me to protect my world which I am sworn to guard?"

Carlos's mother took over at this point.

20

"Marta, Carlos has a device, an instrument which will provide us with your genetic profile, your DNA so we can present that information to the proper authorities and insure that your world will not be harmed as we build a friendship between our races."

"Mistress, I do not understand?"

The Baroness took several minutes explaining DNA to Marta with Carlos bringing up a holographic image of a DNA strain on his cockpit monitor.

"Mistress, I believe I understand now. Thank you for teaching me. I will allow Carlos to take my DNA for you."

Carlos went back into the cabin and retrieved his pocket Doc and once back on the command deck, he linked it to the crystal. He gently took her left hand and placed a finger on the screen. She uttered a surprise and made what could be called a giggle as she watched the lights on the device flicker then turn green. He released her hand and she looked at it, finding nothing different than before.

"Carlos, that felt odd. My finger is not harmed, but it felt as if something was touching it."

"I know Marta, it was the probe within the device taking your DNA. Mother what else do you need?"

"Carlos, we need a full body holographic scan."

"Sure, give me a minute. Marta, please stand and let me move the chair so we can get a view of your complete body."

Marta stood as Carlos bent over and released the clamps on the chair and moved it back out of the way. He then had Marta slowly turn around twice so the view his parents were receiving showed her entire body from the knees up. When his mother advised Carlos they had a good recording of her, he moved the chair back and asked Marta to sit back down. His father took over the conversation at this point as his mother ran a DNA comparison through her computer.

"Marta, we will need to talk with your people. Someone who is in charge, a position of authority on your world."

"Baron, I am responsible for this world. There is only me."

"Father, if I understood Marta correctly, this is a reserve. She told me she was the Warder of this world. This is not her home world."

"Marta is Carlos correct?" His father asked.

"Yes Baron, he is correct."

"Alright. Marta, we can still protect the world you are responsible for, but we will also need to make contact, communicate with your home world so they too can be protected."

"Baron, I am not understanding all of this, but maybe Carlos can explain. This world which I am responsible for is one of many we protect. Can your people protect all of them?"

"Once we know the area which these worlds are in, yes, we can protect them."

"This is confusing, but if I understand your language, I must have faith in what you say to make friends with you and your people."

"Close enough Marta."

Carlos's mother reentered the conversation but this time using Hayutan instead of Fed Speak.

"Carlos, according to her DNA, she is human. A mutant without a doubt, but still human."

Marta turned to look at Carlos.

"I do not understand these words your mother spoke."

"It's alright Marta. It was not fair of mother to speak in our native language, but what she told me was very favorable to you and your people."

"Marta are their many like you on your home world?" Carlos's mother asked.

"Yes, Mistress, and there are others, different from me. We are.... a very diverse people." Marta had paused to find the right words.

"Carlos," His father spoke up. "We need to get things moving on our end. Later we can discuss how and where Marta learned Fed Speak, but put her on the computer to gain a better grasp of our language, so we do not have any misunderstandings. Marta, it is an honor to have met you this day. Please attend to the language lessons which Carlos can provide you and we shall talk again."

"Yes Baron, I shall attend to the lessons."

"Oh, and one last thing Carlos. As your mother was speaking I did a quick check of ships near the rim. I am going to order that Fleet to form a picket line, four parsecs from your current location with instructions to prevent any further exploration into the region until a Federation Team can arrive and begin negotiations with Marta's people."

"I understand Father and thank you."

"One last thing Marta. What do you call your people? Your race?"

"Baron, we are just known as the people."

"Fair enough Marta. Signing off."

Suddenly it was just Carlos and Marta in the ship.

"Marta, I am going to go get my things we left in the forest. Do you wish to start your lessons now?"

She sat for a moment thinking.

"Carlos this is happening very quickly for me to understand all of it. But I do have a question for you."

"Ask it Marta, I'll try to be as honest as I can be."

"When I was out. Lying on your bed. Why didn't you violate me?"

Carlos kneeled down beside her and took her hand in his.

"Marta, I'm sure the contact your people has had with mine has been terrible. Did the slavers violate the females, your people, when they first came?"

"Yes, they did according to our records. Several of our females even became with child because of that violation. It was… what is the word? Horrible for them. And the children they brought forth were disfigured according to our records."

"We'll talk about those children later, but to answer your question, it is not an honorable thing for a man to violate a female. We call it rape and it is an evil thing, yet there are men who would rape you, violate you if they had the chance. But a man of honor only takes that which is given to him. You did not give yourself to me, so I did not take what was not given to me. Do you understand what I am saying?"

"Yes, I think I do. Carlos, I removed all of your clothing to be certain you could not hurt me. Do I need to say something to make that better?"

"No Marta, it is fine as I understand your situation. You said you were all alone here on this world. How is that?"

"This is the way of our life. Yes, I am alone but before I came to you I sent a message to my people. Others will be here in seventeen settings of the sun."

"Then we need to get you better educated in our language and prepare for them as we try to determine which path we shall take in becoming friends."

She tilted her head as she thought about her next words.

"Carlos, I am unknown to the males of my race, but I am bespoken to another. When my time is complete here, I shall return and be his bond mate."

"Then we need to make sure you return as a hero to your people, so your bond mate will be proud of you."

"Thank you. I shall go with you now to collect your things, then you can teach me how to speak better."

Neither spoke as they walked to where his gear was laid out on the ground. Once they had everything picked up with Carlos putting everything back where it belonged he finally asked her a question he had in the back of his mind.

"Marta, how do you travel from place to place in your duties?"

"I have a Sky Rider. It is not far from here. I shall retrieve it and bring it to your ship."

Carlos watched her walk away to get her transport thinking he had to be careful around this new race as they spoke a crude form of Fed Speak and did not have a good understanding of it. He returned to his ship and reconnected with his parents.

"Mother, I have a few minutes alone here. What did you mean when you said that Marta was human?"

"Carlos, the DNA says she is human, but without further samples and hours of examination, I am willing to say her DNA has been altered, somewhat like Centaurians, to give her the appearance she presents."

"Could this be a failed Hayutan experiment?"

"That I cannot say. I've sent the scan to the Altairian Genetic Ministry asking for assistance in reviewing this situation. If possible, try to get another sample for examination and if you can get samples from other individuals, that will help."

"I'll do what I can, but even though she seems trusting at this time, I suspect that is only a front, an act so she can determine if we are as peaceful as I try to project."

"Just be careful Carlos."

"I shall Mother."

Carlos went back into the ship's cabin and opened a concealed panel, then removed a device he was given to help protect his person if he felt it was needed. A device long since considered to have been banned by the Federation yet held in secrecy by the Hayutans. He clipped it too his belt, then got ready to meet Marta upon her return.

He was standing at the foot of the ramp when she returned on an odd looking machine. A machine which did not seem to have a propulsion system yet flew without hardly a sound. Four long struts folded out as she neared the ground and it settled softly. Marta was sitting on what almost appeared to be a saddle with a control stick where a saddle horn would normally be located. Carlos waited until she was off the vehicle before approaching.

She took a bag off a hook on the vehicle and held it up to him.

"I collected something to eat as I walked to get my Sky Rider as the sun is high above us."

Carlos was unsure how to respond, but remembered that when dealing with an unknown culture, try to avoid insulting their daily habits.

"Thank you, Marta."

She then took a small pack from the place it was hanging and walked over to where Carlos's ship was providing some shade. Carlos just watched as she removed a small pot and what appeared to be a stove from the pack, then dumped the contents of the bag on the ground. It was full of fruits and vegetables. Going back to her vehicle, she retrieved a canteen.

Carlos watched as she prepared the items for the pot, placing them in it then adding water from her canteen before putting it on the small stove. Soon the water was boiling even though Carlos could not see any flame from the stove. He watched as she took powders from her pack and sprinkled different ones into the water and stirred the pots contents, mixing the powders in. The fragrance emanating from the pot smell delicious.

"Marta, there is much we must learn about each other's people, so if I ask you questions which you feel are improper, not right, please tell me so I will not make that mistake again."

"I understand Carlos. I have those same …. thoughts."

Carlos could tell she was searching to find the right words with her meager understanding of his language.

"Marta on a world full of animals, do you eat meat?"

"Oh no Carlos, that is forbidden. We females only consume what the dirt provides us."

"Excuse me Marta, you said we females. Does that mean your men, the males consume meat?"

"Yes, they take the flesh of animals, so they can be strong, so they can produce many offspring."

"Interesting. Thank you, Marta."

"Do you take of the animal?"

"Yes, Marta, as does our females. If you will forgive me, I shall go get something to eat from my ship."

27

"There is enough here for you also. Or does it not please you?"

"It smells very good Marta, I did not want to take from you is all."

She was quiet for a moment as he figured she was searching for the words she needed to speak.

"I gathered enough for the two of us to consume."

"Thank you."

He looked at her things laid out and did not see any bowls, only a single cup and the pot she was cooking in. He excused himself and went into the ship and retrieve two bowls and spoons plus a container of fruit juice along with a cup for himself. When he returned, he sat the things down then poured a bit of juice in her cup, then some in his own, taking a sip of it so she could see him consume it. She looked at the bowls and it seemed she blushed.

"When I take nourishment, I take it from the…." She thought for a moment then tapped the side of the pot with her spoon.

"It's a pot Marta, and these are bowls." He held a bowl up, so she would know what he was referencing.

"Pot. Bowls. I have much to learn."

She soon felt the soup was ready and she carefully poured equal portions in the bowls before trying the juice Carlos had poured for her. She smiled at the taste, and he filled her cup for her.

His first taste of the hot soup was what he considered the best soup he had ever tasted and told her so. As they ate, she asked him about his world and he did his best to be as honest and replied in as simple terms as possible. But he felt she was becoming frustrated with her lack on knowledge of his language.

Carlos was amazed that a few short hours before she had him hanging nude as if she was ready to skin him. He was grateful for the security system his parents had insisted he have in his ship and their ability to activate it, thus rescuing him from her control. He also felt he had made the right decision not to tie her up or take away her weapons.

Deep inside though, Carlos was afraid he was being played by this female. He had tricked her and subdued her, then exposed her to technology she acted as if she had never seen before. And he had even greater technology at his fingertips he was not about to expose to her such as the spoon he was using to gently stir his soup with.

The spoon looked like any other spoon found in any home across the universe except it had micro-sensors built into it to detect poisons or agents which might cause a human harm. If it detected harmful agents in the soup, the face of the spoon's handle would turn a soft red. The spoon was actually part of the Fleet's Survival Kit to prevent an individual stranded on an unknown planet from eating something which might do them harm. His spoon never turned colors.

He asked her about the vegetables in the soup and how to find them. Marta told him she would show him the next time she gathered them. It was over the soup that Carlos was able to convince Marta to change locations, move to her habitat, so she would have access to her communications with her home world and other aspects of her daily life on this world.

Her habitat was actually a cave with a large opening capable of holding her Sky Rider, which she flew into and landed. This was why he had not detected her during his orbital survey as it was located in a region heavy with iron and he had basically dismissed any anomalies in the sensor readings as extraneous minerals in the soil.

He never asked to examine her habitat, but told her that the next day, she could start her language lessons. But he did tell her she should notify her home world of the situation between them so when he people arrived, they would not land as an attacking force.

That evening, secure in his ship, Carlos spoke with his parents again, advising them of what he had learned up to that time. His father advised him to keep as many secrets as possible and to take every precaution possible to insure his safety. Carlos was also told that the Fleet would be on station within eight solar days, and that they would contact him when on station.

Learning Curve

Carlos quickly discovered that Marta was smarter than she at first seemed as she sat for hours in front of the cockpit computer learning the language in depth. If she had trouble understanding a word or phrase, even with the computer's guidance, she would ask him to further explain the concept.

By the time the Fleet notified him they were on station, Marta had a good grasp of Fed Speak and their conversations became more technical as she wanted to know about his ship and life on other worlds.

Carlos would go out with Marta to collect the fruits and vegetables she ate and he would also shared his rations with her, insuring she only ate the vegetable portions of the rations in keeping with her world's customs of the females avoiding eating meat. But it was during one mid-day meal that he learned more about her own life and the future it held.

"Carlos, as you know, I am bespoken, pledged to a great warrior. His name is Moshe, and he has faced those you call a slaver in battle. It is an honor to become a member of his Harem."

"He has other wives?"

"Oh yes. I will be wife number five. When I last spoke to him, he had eleven off spring by the other wives, but of that only two males to carry his bloodline forward. He hopes I will give him male off spring instead of females. It is one of the reasons he sought me out and bargained with my father for his bed."

Carlos had to bite his tongue to keep from telling her about the genetics of off spring, in that it was the male who determined such things, not the females. Then it was the phrase bargained for which really upset him. She was property, not a person, which was something the Federation would have to address.

31

She had shown him her habitat, and with the technology it contained, she should have been considered an equal, but by her own words, she was not in their society. But it was not his place to challenge those perceptions within their society.

"Marta, how is it that you are here, isolated from your world on this one if you are to be mated with another?"

"I am here so I will not mate with one I am not pledged too."

"How long have you been here, on this world?"

"Six annuals. I am now prime for mating and will soon return to my world and bond with Moshe."

"How old are you?"

"I am eighteen annuals, excuse me, years by our method of keeping dates. How old are you by your method?"

"I am twenty-eight years old by my calendar."

She sat for a long time stirring her soup as she seemed to be in thought.

"Carlos, I sense there is much you are not telling me about your world and I can accept that. We have started a new life, and a new relationship between worlds and I am not the proper one to do this. Neither of us truly trusts the other one but we are in a position to gain further trust or destroy what we have built so far."

"Yes Marta, there is much more to be learned about each other's worlds, but that is for the diplomats to deal with, not the two of us. But after a rough meeting between us, I think we can become solid friends."

"I think so too Carlos. Carlos, when I had you nude, hanging from the tree, I took your manhood in hand and held it. I have never seen a male's manhood and wondered what it was going to feel like having it in me to give me the seed to produce an off spring."

She was blushing as she spoke.

"That's alright Marta, but it is not wise to speak of such things, especially since you are pledged to another."

"Carlos, my coverings were intact when I awoke telling me that you did not view my private parts and that you had not violated me. I felt ashamed at what I did to you."

"Stripping me of my clothing was an act to protect yourself. What else you did was being curious as I am the first human you have met."

Something about the way she looked at him told Carlos she was once more hiding something from him. But he changed the subject to her language lessons and they spent some time with her trying to teach him their language. He had trouble wrapping his tongue around some of the way the words were spoken but he was slowly getting a grasp of the language itself, even if he was having trouble speaking it.

She expressed her desire to learn more of his language and after the meal, he showed her how to queue up the course in the computer and just left her alone. Marta had already learned how to access definitions if she did not understand a word or phrase, so he was not needed to assist her.

Late the next morning, Carlos was working on his Pad when Marta came out of the cockpit and just looked at him. He returned her gaze and felt she was upset, but he had a faint idea what she was upset with considering the subject she was studying.

"Yes Marta?"

"Carlos, I was interested in this DNA that your mother spoke of and looked it up on the computer. I read about how it acts between male and female. Does that mean the off spring I give to Moshe will be determined by him, not by me?"

"Yes Marta, it does. It is that way all over the universe, with all manner of animals of which even humans are a form of animal."

"But it is possible I could give him sons?"

"Again, yes Marta, you could since he has sired two sons already, it is possible, but from what you have told me, it is more likely you will give him female off spring."

"Do you have off spring?"

"No Marta, I do not. I have never bonded with another even though I have bedded several in my short life. Humans are not as restricted in mating with each other without being bonded. But both subjects take precautions not to bring forth off spring."

"When I spoke of being pledged to Moshe, you already knew about this DNA, and what may happen between Moshe and myself."

"Yes, Marta, I did, and I should have locked you out from that part of the computer. I wish you had not seen that information."

She cocked her head as she often did when thinking.

"Did you say this, so you could have me?"

"No Marta, I did not. It was a serious mistake on my part. I'm sorry."

She just looked at him for a moment before returning to the cockpit and her lessons. When he called her to the mid-day meal, she took her bowl and went outside and sat in the sun as she ate without speaking to him. After she ate, she cleaned her bowl then left the ship and went into her habitat. Carlos took a chair outside and just waited in the shade on his ship as he read from his pad.

It was past the normal time for the evening meal when she came from her habitat and just stood in front of him.

"Carlos, I have received a message saying there are ships out in space just floating there between your worlds and mine. Are they the ships your father mentioned?"

"Yes, Marta, they are. They are there to prevent any other humans from entering your space until we can agree on a treaty."

"A treaty is a pledge of friendship between our worlds?"

"Yes, that and other things, but mostly friendship."

"Moshe and others will be here in six days. I will send a message telling my people the ships in space are there to prevent any more humans from coming to our worlds until an agreement can be made between your worlds and mine."

Marta looked at him for a moment before continuing.

"Carlos, I have been told that I can kill you if I feel you are lying to me. Moshe even sent me a message for me to kill you before you can violate me. I have the ability to do that Carlos, but inside, I think what you have said to me is with honor. I will not kill you, but when Moshe arrives, I suspect he will try to kill you as he has much hate in his soul for humans."

She turned on her heel before Carlos could respond and disappeared inside her habitat. Carlos left his chair and went into his ship and fixed a meal and took it back outside and just waited.

As the sun set, Carlos went back inside his ship and sealed it as he sat down and recorded a verbal report to be sent to his parents on the events of the day. He reported what Marta had said about killing him and Moshe's hatred for humans. He reviewed his report then tied it to his crystal and sent it to his parents knowing his mother would be upset by his actions. Carlos searched his own feelings concerning Marta and could not determine anything more than the desire to be a good friend to her even though in many ways, she was a desirable female. But even if his mother had declared Marta human, she was an alien. An alien whose culture was as foreign to him as his was to her. He held no bias concerning her race or appearance, it was just that he did not feel any attraction to her.

The next morning, Carlos found Marta squatting at the end of the ship's ramp waiting for him. She stood and was clear in what she wanted from him.

"Carlos, I learned that I can have my DNA compared to those kept in the computer data files. Your mother spoke to you in an unknown language when she received my DNA and I want to know what she said or saw. Will you grant me this wish?"

"Yes Marta, I will grant you that wish, but you may not like what you discover. Are you sure you want to do this?"

"Carlos, I already dislike what I have discovered, but let me be clear in that I will fulfill my obligation to my family and bond with Moshe, even if what I have learned is true."

Carlos never responded to her comment, only motioned her to enter the ship and then into the cockpit where he took her DNA sample and entered it into the computer. He accessed the DNA Comparison program then left the cockpit, so she would have privacy as she reviewed the file once complete.

When Marta exited the ship, she just walked out then sat down on the ground, looking towards the plains out in front of where they were located. She sat for a long time before speaking without looking at Carlos.

"Carlos, I can never speak of this to my people as they will never believe me. I'm not sure that even I believe what I have read. How can I trust that it is the truth and not some information planted in your computer to challenge our way of thinking about ourselves?"

"Marta, I am truly sorry. I started with the idea teaching you my language so you could help your people engage with my people and develop a friendship to last for generations. When you came to me, and I posted the message about your people, I lost all that I had found here. The riches of this world vanished at the end of my fingertips, but those riches mean nothing to me if I could help your people join with mine. Have I lost that too?"

"No Carlos, you haven't, but you also know that the females of my people have very little power. I've read your Principles of Leadership and even though I do not completely understand them, your people holds females as equals. You even have a female in power as the supreme leader of your universe."

"Yes, Princess Constance is our guiding light so to speak. She is a kind and just ruler having taken the Throne from her father who was also a firm, but just ruler."

"Carlos, I read that. The former leader was named Gannaway such as you. Is this important to me?"

"Marta, Princess Constance is my aunt, sister to my father. Prince Ismael is my Grandfather, my ancestor. My father is a Baron as you already know, and I am his heir. I am known as Earl Carlos Gannaway to my people."

"If what I read was true, then you have power and privilege. Why did you come out here into this space without another to help you?"

"I came to find my own riches, my own place in the universe instead of just being another in a long line of powerful family. Even the small percentage the Federation would allow me to keep from the riches of this world once it was opened to settlement would surpass what I already have from my family. I wanted to be separate from my family's wealth and lay claim to my own."

"I still have much to learn Carlos, and I am not sure I have the strength or intelligence to learn especially in the short time we have here. I must warn you that Moshe and the others will not take kindly to you being here."

"Marta, I shall be cautious in dealing with Moshe and the others, but if that was a subtle hint for me to leave, I shall not go and leave you alone to deal with Moshe in this matter. My family is cursed with the duty that is often forced upon us. I shall not run away for others to deal with your people until my people order me away from here."

"Why was it important to you that I become educated? To learn your language better?"

"So you could help your people join with mine. Marta, I understand parts of your language now, but you have a much better grasp of ours than I shall ever have of yours."

Marta returned to the ship and continued her language lessons, improving her skills and knowledge.

That evening, Carlos contacted the Hayutan Cruiser Endeavor after Marta had left for the night. He asked for a full section of Centaurian Marines equipped with personal cloaking devices and an Assault Boat also so equipped to be standing by in case of need. He asked that the section be made up of male and female, and they were to carry their blades to the planet if called for.

Two hours later he received approval from the Throne via his father to utilize the Centaurians. Now all he could do was wait until Moshe and company arrived.

Carlos did not push conversation with Marta during the days they had left as she increased her language skills with the computer and from time to time ventured onto other subjects that caught her interest. She took her morning and evening meals in her habitat, while sharing a meal with him during the mid-day that he prepared.

The Centaurians landed late the night before Marta's people took an orbit over the planet and Carlos briefed them on what he expected them to do during the first hours of meeting Moshe and the others. While cloaked they were to pair up with her people and be ready to disarm them if things turned violent. He expressed that they were to take every precaution possible to prevent major injuries to these people and that they had experienced contact with slavers meaning their first reactions could be dangerous.

Carlos showed the Centaurians a hologram of Marta and explained that because of her genetic appearance, it was why he had asked for only Centaurians for this mission.

Just before daylight, Marta requested entrance into the ship. She was dressed differently this morning in that she was wearing a bright orange kilt with a matching vest over her normal leather coverings. Her long knife was present along with what she said was a communications device. Marta advised Carlos that Moshe would be landing just after sunrise.

Carlos dressed in his Fleet uniform with the rank of Lieutenant Commander on his collars but decided not to wear his helmet this day. Instead he wore a tiny communications headset which he had already checked to insure he could talk to the Centaurians with. He laid his swords out on his bunk telling Marta they were part of his uniform, but he would leave his sidearm in the ship, showing her he had put it away.

But also on his belt was his own cloaking device, placed so it would seem natural for him to have his hand on it as he planned to be ready to disappear if the situation became dangerous dealing with Moshe.

All they could do was wait as orbit information was being fed to him via the headset from the Assault Boat. As they stood outside the ship watching the ship carrying Moshe land, Carlos put on a pair of tinted glasses telling Marta that the sun was bothering his eyes this morning and the glasses were to protect them when in fact these glasses let him see the cloaked Centaurians.

As the small ship descended to land, Marta spoke up once again.

"Carlos, I should hate you, but I don't. You have opened my eyes to a universe I never knew and in doing so makes me hate the one I have. I shall go with Moshe and give him children, so I do not dishonor my family, but if I had a choice, I would stay with you. Not because I have feelings for you, but so I could learn more about the vast universe."

"I'm sorry Marta that I have done this to you. But now you can work to open your people to the universe."

"Carlos, they will never allow a female to be more than what they think we are. We are servants, slaves to bear children for the males of my race. Once we separate, you and I will never see each other again, and I will never have another chance to study the universe as you have allowed me too."

Carlos never responded to her as he knew things were being planned that would once again allow them to see each other and speak to each other as equals. But he did have a question he had never asked and knew he had a short time to ask it.

"Marta, you once said that the slavers breed with females of your race and produced deformed off spring. How were they deformed?"

"They were covered in fur as I am, but their faces were human such as yours, and they had no tails."

Carlos stifled a laugh as she had just described a Centaurian.

"What happened to those children?"

"They were taken to another world such as this one and given the means to live and be the warders of that world."

"It looks like Moshe and company are about to land. Marta, I have enjoyed your company and wish you all the best your world has to offer."

"Thank you, Carlos."

Confrontation

As the small ship settled on its landing struts, Carlos could see the Centaurians move in on the ship, waiting to pick up the people who disembark. Soon a hatch opened, and a ramp came down and men began to move down the ramp. The first male was all black with a large mane of hair with two knives at his waist and a staff in his right hand. He was a large male and looked as if he could handle himself in a fight.

"That is Moshe." Marta advised him.

"Thought that might be. Thank you."

The Centaurians began to pair off with the other eight men who left the ship behind Moshe, staying slightly behind and to the side of each man. Two stayed at the hatch ready to board the ship if necessary. The rest of the section just spread out to provide cover for the others if needed.

While the other men used their staffs to assist in walking, Moshe had his at his side, somewhat level with the ground as if he was expecting to use it. At about fifty meters he moved his staff, holding it in both hands such as Marta did when she knocked Carlos out with the pulse she fired at him. Carlos noticed he twisted the staff which panicked Marta and she stepped in front of Carlos.

Marta was calling out to Moshe in her own language which Carlos could barely understand as she moved further in front of him, holding her hands out as if to stop Moshe. Moshe kept coming and Carlos could see the look on his face was one of hatred.

She was about two meters in front of Carlos when Moshe stepped up to her and growled as he swung on her with his left hand, hitting Marta in the head with the back of his fist, knocking her to the ground as he stepped to Carlos. Carlos pushed the button on his cloaking device.

As the cloak took effect, Carlos took a step forward and to the right of Moshe, as Moshe once more took a grip on his staff but found he had no target. As Carlos stepped to Moshe's side, he pulled his Katana and sliced through Moshe's staff near where it was being held. Carlos must have ruptured the staff's power pack as it seemed to explode in sparks, knocking Moshe back and to the ground with his fur being singed.

Carlos looked at Marta, lying on the ground, moving, trying to get up, then he looked down at Moshe who was dazed from the power surge of his ruptured power pack. Noise from the others caused Carlos to take a quick look to see two of the others going down from being struck in the back of the head by the butts of the Centaurians carbines, and another having his staff ripped from his hands.

He turned his attention back to Moshe who was trying to draw one of his knives while on the ground. Carlos turned off his cloak and held the tip of his Katana slightly above Moshe's face. Moshe's eyes widened as Carlos suddenly appeared and the polished tip of the sword was nearly close enough to shave him.

"Marta, are you alright?"

"Carlos, please do not kill him!"

"I have no intention of killing him unless he makes another attempt to harm me. Tell him that."

Marta spoke to Moshe, then to Carlos.

"Carlos, he knows your language as I knew it when we first met."

"Good, but you will translate what I say to him, so he and I will have an understanding. Moshe do you understand that?"

"Yes human, I understand."

"Good. I came to this world in peace and mean no creature any harm, but be warned, if I see you strike Marta again, I will remove the hand you strike her with. Translate Marta so he understands."

"Carlos, I can't."

"Marta, translate or I will harm him to insure he understands me."

She spoke to Moshe and he replied back to her.

"He understands Carlos."

"Moshe, in my world, our females are respected, honored, not used as servants to be treated as inferiors. Translate Marta."

She did as she was told. Moshe replied directly to Carlos.

"This is not your world human, and you do not tell us what we can do."

Carlos was quick with his sword and slapped Moshe in the crotch with the flat of the blade. Moshe jerked and grabbed his groin as the pain erupted from his groin.

"Moshe do not think I am afraid of you. If you wish to challenge me with knives, I will gladly face you."

Moshe looked up at Carlos and realized this was not like the humans he had faced before. This human did not fear him. He turned his head to look at Marta who was still on the ground and spoke to her in their language. She replied to him.

"Marta, I did not understand all of that, what did he say to you?"

"He asked me if you had touched me. Violated me. I told him you were an honorable man and had not touched me."

Moshe slowly moved so he could see the other men in his group and was confused that two were down and the others were looking around, trying to find the cause.

Carlos laughed, then called out for two of the female Centaurians to attend him. These were two females in their traditional dance attire of knee high black boots, black leather thong and a black leather halter along with the traditional black half-mask over their heads. They moved to Carlos's side and uncloaked. One of the females was a cinnamon, and the other a blond.

"What is this? Moshe cried out.

"These females are from my world. They are called Centaurians, and they are fierce warriors. If you wish to face me with knives, they will insure no one interferes in our battle."

Moshe had a puzzled look on his face. Marta translated what Carlos had said, then spoke to Carlos.

"Carlos, you were alone when we met."

"Yes Marta, but I was not going to meet your people without protection. And it is because I have these friends, that Moshe is still alive. If I was alone, I would already have killed him and the men who came with him. Tell me he was not going to kill me when he struck you."

She never answered his question, only sat on the ground with her head down.

"Stand Moshe, I'm tired of looking down at you." Carlos commanded.

Moshe slowly stood and let out a light moan as his groin was still aching from the smack of Carlos's blade. He looked at Carlos with a snare on his lips.

"Human, I am not afraid of you and the females you have with you. I could kill you now without effort and my men would enjoy your females."

There was a noise to their side where Moshe's men were standing, and another man went down, this time shaking as he lay on the ground. Carlos figured one of the Centaurians had shot the man with an Electro-dart.

"What were you saying Moshe about your men using the females? Shall I step aside and allow you to attempt to take either of my friends? They do have claws of their own."

Both Centaurian females drew their sword from over their shoulders and just let them hang at their sides.

"Ha! Those do not scare me. Females with useless blades that they would hurt themselves with."

Carlos stepped aside, allowing the Centaurians full access to Moshe.

"Vanna, give Moshe a demonstration and try not to draw blood if possible."

The blond Centaurian laughed as her blades began a swirling movement in front of her as she also stepped closer to Moshe. He tried to follow the blade action, but it was happening too fast for him to keep up with when Vanna closed to him then stepped back, letting her blades once more rest beside her.

Moshe looked down at his body and saw pieces of his fur falling to the ground, then three of the leather cross straps on his body fell away, neatly cut apart while he was not touched by the tips of Vanna's blades.

As this was happening, Carlos had softly spoken into his headset mic for all of the Centaurians to decloak. Moshe looked at Carlos, then at his own men to see he was surrounded by armed men and women, all of which were covered in fur.

"Who are these creatures Human? They appear to be like the spawn of our females who were violated by humans."

"Moshe, they are called Centaurians and they are as human as I am, only they have their fur, where I have none. They are great warriors, and some say the females are more dangerous than the males. Marta, make sure Moshe understands what I am about to say to him."

"Yes Carlos."

"Moshe, you will return to your ship and send the following message to your world. To your leaders."

Marta translated for him.

"We come in peace and offer our friendship to your people. We offer protection to your worlds from those that would enslave your people."

Marta once again translated.

"My people, the Federation of Planets wish to meet with your leaders and form a treaty between our worlds for peaceful co-existence."

Marta again translated for Carlos.

"Tell them I shall wait here on this world for their message. I shall not take from this world and I shall keep it as it is. Marta will go with you to ensure you send the message I gave you and will return to tell me it has been done."

Marta looked up at Carlos before translating.

"Moshe, Marta is pledged to your house and I must respect that pledge, but she will stay in her habitat until you leave this world and that will not be until I have received a reply to my message."

"Carlos, you cannot do this."

"Marta, I can and will. Translate please."

She did as she was told, and Carlos could see Moshe becoming upset once again. Moshe growled a low growl but held his tongue.

"Moshe, if you attempt to leave this world, you will be stopped. I came in peace and you tried to kill me. In my world, I could take your head and show it to the universe, but as I said before, it is because I consider Marta a friend, I will let you keep your head, but do not test me Moshe as I do not need my allies to remove your head from your body."

Marta translated as Carlos made a show of flipping his Katana and slipping it back into its scabbard. Carlos then walked past Moshe over to Marta and offered his hand to her to help her up off the ground. He looked at the side of her head where she had been hit and saw blood on her ear. Carlos ran his finger into the blood and looked at it then at Moshe.

"We do not treat our females in such a fashion. They give us children, warmth in our beds, and companionship. They are not property to be treated with such disrespect."

Carlos walked back to Moshe and wiped the blood from his finger onto Moshe's chest.

"Pull your claws in Moshe or I will forget my promise to Marta not to kill you this day. Now go, do as I said and send the message back to your home world."

Moshe glared at Carlos for a minute then growl to Marta in their language as he turned to his ship. Carlos stopped him.

"Wait. Use Marta's communications device in her habitat. Sabrina and Vanna will accompany you to see that you do as instructed."

"Human, you force these deformed ones on me?"

"Yes Moshe, I force them on you and they are not deformed, only different, just as you are different than me. Now, do as I say before I forget my promise to Marta not to kill you."

Sabrina spoke to Carlos in Hayutan.

"Rules of engagement Lord Carlos?"

"None at all Lieutenant."

"Fair enough."

Marta looked at Carlos as he had also spoken in Hayutan without her understanding. Moshe responded instead of her.

"What tongue did you speak to the female?"

"It was the tongue, the language of my birth. She asked for guidance in escorting you, and I gave her what I felt was right. Now go, I am getting tired of looking at you."

Moshe walked past Carlos as Marta followed him without looking at Carlos. The Centaurians followed close behind with their swords in their sheaths. Carlos took a deep breath and just watched as they entrance the cave where Marta had her quarters. He reached up and touched his headset.

"Father, did you receive everything?"

Instead of his father's voice, he heard a woman's voice, a voice he did not expect to hear.

"Carlos, I commend you for not killing or injuring that individual named Moshe."

Carlos closed his eyes for a moment before answering.

"Your Highness, I felt it was the best option at the moment, but I feel I made a mistake in not killing him. I fear for Marta's safety."

"Carlos, what about Marta?" It was his father.

"Father, she has been a good companion and no, I have not touched her other than offering my hand to her. But she is bright, intelligent and has learned Fed Speak very well, along with other things within the universe. From talking with her, the females are nothing more than servants, slaves to produce children and the males believe it is the female which controls the sex of their children."

"Yes, Carlos, we have read your reports." Once again it was his Aunt, the Princess Consuela responding. "What are you plans now, Carlos?"

"I hope to hold them here until someone of authority responds and talks can begin. I'm hopefully those that respond will not have the hate inside them that Moshe has."

"Lord Earl Carlos Gannaway of Hollis, the Throne requires that you attend to the opening of these new worlds with patience and self-control while acting as the direct representative of the Throne. There should be a diplomatic group at your location within ten standard days to assist in your efforts."

"Your Highness, I shall do my best to control my emotions and represent the Throne on your behalf."

"Carlos, one final thing. The Throne recognizes that these people may be what can best be called bullies. People who use fear to get what they desire. I will not tie your hands in dealing with them in that arena, but use your best judgement on how far to go. Those instructions may be open ended, but I have faith you will use restraint in such matters."

Carlos softly laughed.

"Your Highness, that was clear as mud, but I understand what your were saying. I shall do my best to maintain my temper in proper fashion."

"One final thing Carlos, I have dispatched two additional Fleets to the area to support your efforts. Use them wisely."

"Yes, Your Highness."

No one spoke after that as Carlos waited until Marta exited the habitat with Moshe following and the Centaurians behind him. Marta walked up to Carlos with her head bowed.

"Lord Carlos, the message has been sent and it was indicated it has been received. Moshe wants me to board his ship and they will leave to take me back to my world."

Carlos looked at Moshe as he walked up to them.

"Moshe, you will stay until we have an answer since Marta speaks my tongue now and to insure no mistakes are made in working out details of further meetings. Marta make sure Moshe understands."

Before Marta could speak, Moshe spoke.

"I understand Human. You want Marta for your bed but she is spoken to me. We leave and bond, then she will give me many sons."

"No Moshe, she is yours upon bonding and I must respect that. But both of you will stay until another can come and sit down and talk about a treaty between our two worlds. Marta will stay in her habitat under the protection of my Centaurians until it is time for you to leave, and not before then."

"You speak false, you want her on your bed."

"Then it will get crowded on Lord Carlos's bed." Sabrina spoke up. "It is only made for two and I will be on his bed this night."

Marta looked at Sabrina, then translated what she said to Moshe who growled at her causing Marta to once more drop her head in submission.

"Lieutenant Sativa, bring the boat in uncloaked."

Sabrina spoke into her headset and within moments, you could hear the sound of the Assault Boat's thrusters. Moshe looked around trying to detect where the sound was coming from when the boat suddenly appeared over the top of his own ship. Moshe crouched as if he was going to ponce, then stood up as he looked at the boat hovering above his. He turned on Carlos.

"What is this magic?"

"It's not magic Moshe, it's science. Do you think you can fight my science?"

Moshe looked back at the Assault Boat which was about half the size of his own ship. The Plasma cannons mounted forward on the sides of the boat were extended and the Plasma turret atop the ship was sweeping back and forth looking for a target.

"Moshe, as I said earlier, do not attempt to lift without my permission. That ship is faster than yours and those cannons will break your ship into pieces. Now go, gather your men and return to your ship and stay there. Vanna, escort Marta to her quarters please."

Moshe growled something to Marta and she froze. Carlos put his hand on his Katana.

"Moshe, go before I forget my promise. Marta, do as I said please."

Moshe turned away and motioned for his men to go to the ship. One of the downed men had recovered and the others helped moved the two unconscious men to the ship. Once they were on the ship, the Assault Boat slipped over and landed between the alien ship and Carlos's ship with its cannons pointed at the alien ship.

Carlos watched as he removed his headset from his ear and just took a deep breath. Sabrina came up beside him and just stood without speaking. He finally broke the silence between them.

"Sabrina, it is good to see you again."

"It is good to see you also Carlos. It has been a long time since we broke bread together."

"Yes it has. Thanks for covering me with the bed thing."

"Well I wasn't exactly covering if you understand my meaning. Unless you would prefer Marta?"

"No Sabrina, Marta is attractive in her own way and regardless of her looks she is as human as you or I. But no, she will never see my bed in such a fashion."

"Then I think tonight would be a good time to get reacquainted with an old friend."

"That's what I always liked about you Sabrina. Your shyness." He looked at her and grinned.

The Wait

The next twenty days, waiting for a representative of Marta's people to arrive was not without problems between Moshe and his men and Carlos's people.

During the first night, two more Assault Boats landed with their sections of Marines and Lancers to provide additional security for Carlos as a Destroyer took orbit above the planet having been ordered there by the Throne. Moshe protested this action and Carlos just listened for several minutes then told Moshe to shut up and go back to his ship.

Three days later one of Moshe's men pushed one of the female Centaurians out of his way and found himself face down in the dirt with a foot on his neck belonging to the female. When the male was finally allowed to stand up, he challenged the female to try that again.

Carlos had an idea knowing the abilities of the female Lancers and required both to remove all weapons and for both to wear gloves knowing the male had retractable claws. The male did not like the idea of the gloves but when the female pulled her gloves on, he gave in and put on a pair provided by one of the male Lancers.

Marta translated the rules of engagement for Carlos so her people would understand how the challenge would be conducted between the two people with her people demanding that the female could not kick the male in the groin. Moshe's ship emptied as they were to witness the fight with the Marines and Lancers insuring none of them had a weapon they could toss to the male against the female.

Karina, the female just stood in the middle of the area they were to fight in and watched as her opponent took a crouched position and began to circle her, looking for the opening to take her down. He came in close to her and she did a spinning heel kick and laid him down with her boot heel connecting with his head. Karina did not follow through and finish him, but allowed him to get up.

Marta was standing between Sabrina and Vanna and quietly spoke without looking away from the action in front of her.

"Peyto is Moshe's best fighter. This is what I think you would call a set-up to show the males are stronger and to put your females in what our males consider their place."

"Marta, then they picked the wrong female to teach that lesson too. Karina, is one of the best hand to hand fighters in the Lancers. She grew up with four older brothers and learned to fight as soon as she could walk." Sabrina replied to Marta's comments.

They watched as Karina swept the legs from under Peyto, causing him to land hard on his back. He rolled over and jumped up, lunging at Karina who moved his arm away and hit him behind the ear as he passed her, putting him once more on the ground.

"Mistress Sabrina, she needs to put Peyto down and keep him down. He is getting angry and will try to kill her if he can. Moshe just called out to him to kill her."

"And you are going to bond with Moshe?"

"It is my world Mistress; my family's honor is at stake."

Neither spoke for several minutes as they watched Karina play with Peyto.

"Mistress Sabrina, you shared Carlos's bed last night."

Sabrina looked at Marta.

"How did you know that Marta?"

"I can smell him on you."

"I bathed this morning; how can you smell Carlos on me?"

"He held you close after. If not for my oath to Moshe, I would have considered his bed."

Sabrina did not respond to Marta's comment as they watch the fight. Karina was abusing Peyto without doing any real damage other than greatly embarrassing him in front of his crew mates.

Karina lost her footing for a second and Peyto was able to get his hands on her. She took him to the ground as she tried to break his grasp. As she was breaking his hold on her, he put his gloved hand in his mouth and pulled the glove off his hands and extended his claws. Just as he was about to take a swipe at her face with his claws, he was hit with an Electro-dart stopping his reach for her and allowing Karina to push him off her.

Moshe and two others stepped forward to assist Peyto to find themselves facing four females with their swords pulled and ready to meet them. They retreated back to their original positions.

Karina rolled up and stepped to Peyto, then pulled the dart from his side. She picked up his glove and just moved back away from him facing the other aliens and waited. Moshe yelled a protest about the dart and Carlos yelled back Peyto violated the rules and pulled his glove off.

It was several minutes before Peyto stirred and sat up, shaking his head. He looked around to see Karina standing well out of reach. She threw his glove at him and motioned for him to put it back on. He put the glove back on then stood on shaking legs as he struggled to get his bearings. Karina just stood, waiting for him to make the next move as Moshe and crew were yelling at him to finish her.

When Peyto finally made his move, Karina met him head on this time not holding a thing back as the sound of breaking bones could be heard mixed with Peyto's howls of pain until he stopped howling and crumpled to the ground.

Karina stood over Peyto's broken body, then looked at the crowd of alien men before spitting on Peyto before moving to her side of the makeshift arena. Two of the aliens moved to Peyto's body and checked him. One spoke to Moshe who became irritated at what he was told. Marta spoke to Sabrina about what was said.

"Peyto is dead. Moshe is upset that a female killed his best fighter with only her hands."

"Marta, Peyto tried to injure or kill Karina with his claws. In our worlds, she had the right to kill him."

Moshe stepped out from the group of his men and pointed to Karina.

"Give her to me!" He demanded as he pointed towards her.

Karina reached over to the Lancer standing next to her and drew his short blade from its sheath and started back into the arena. Carlos's voice echoed across the field.

"Back away Specialists." He ordered as he walked into the arena.

He pulled his Katana and stuck it into the ground then his short sword beside it before continuing to face Moshe. He stopped well out of arms reach of Moshe.

"Peyto violated the rules of the fight and has paid for his mistake."

Moshe looked at Carlos trying to find the words then looked over to Marta and growled at her. Marta moved to them so she could translate with Sabrina following close behind. Moshe spoke to Marta then Marta looked at Carlos.

"Moshe says that the fight was interfered with when Peyto was shot with the dart. He was weakened and could not defend himself."

"Moshe, Peyto removed his glove and extended his claws to strike Karina. The dart only caused him not to harm her with his claws. The female, Karina waited until he recovered and waited until he attacked her before killing him. She followed the rules of engagement of our code of honor. Peyto could have walked away but he did not. His death is on him. Translate please Marta."

Marta translated for Carlos and Moshe snapped at her, causing her to slightly step back from him. Carlos reached behind his back and pulled a large knife, a Bowie knife made decades before by his ancestor, Prince Harshal.

"Moshe, would you like to fight me? You can use your claws and a knife."

Marta started to translate with Moshe interrupting her.

"I understand his words."

Moshe stood looking at Carlos and the large knife as he thought about the challenge. He decided that if a human female was as deadly as the one who killed Peyto, then the males must be even more dangerous.

"No human, I will not fight you."

He turned away and walked back to the others and then moved to their ship with Peyto's body being carried by two of the aliens.

Carlos never spoke to Marta as he moved back to his swords and returned them to their sheaths. The Lancers and Marines broke up and moved to positions where they could watch the ship without being bunched up. Carlos turned back to his ship and watched as Marta returned to her habitat with Vanna following behind her. Sabrina intercepted him as he walked to his ship.

"You took a great risk Carlos, challenging him that way."

"Maybe, but he knew he would not survive if he had accepted the challenge. I might have received a few claw marks, but he would have died just the same."

"Yes, he would have. Marta told me as we watched the fight that if she was not pledged to Moshe, she would have considered your bed. This is after she told me she could smell you on me from when we kissed before leaving the ship. Are you going to allow her to go away with that monster?"

"We have no choice in the matter Sabrina. But I'll not lie and say that was not part of the consideration when I challenged Moshe. If I had killed him, I would have freed her from her pledge, and not, it was not so I could take her to my bed."

Marta stayed in her habitat unless called for or had to go forage for food. One of the Kats, as the Centaurians had started referring to them, asked to do some hunting to supplement their own food supply. Carlos allowed them to hunt but never when Marta was out foraging.

Through Marta translating, they asked to go further away to hunt for larger animals. Carlos had an air car brought down from the Destroyer, and three Marines took one of the Kats, named Malloc, to where a herd of cattle like creatures were grazing. They returned with a gutted cow suspended from the air car and Malloc excited about having flown in the air car.

A large pit was dug and a fire built by the Centaurians where they suspended half the cow on a spit and began cooking it as the other half was taken into the Kat's ship for them to eat. Marta showed where to find vegetables to go with the meat and a large pot was placed at the edge of the fire to cook the mixture of vegetables.

That evening as the humans were slicing large pieces off the carcass, several of the Kats were sitting outside their ship and watched. When they saw the female humans also eating the meat, they protested saying meat was only for the males. One of the non-Centaurian females invited the males to try and prevent her from eating the meat. Nothing more was said about this breach in the Kat's culture.

After several days on the planet, the off duty Marines and Lancers began exercising as a group since they now had room to run and extend their normal ship board exercises while on the planet. The Kats watched this happening and after a couple days, they also began doing exercises, but Moshe was rarely seen outside his ship.

One morning, the Marines were practicing hand to hand combat and a couple of the Kats watched then tried to imitate what they were seeing. One of the Marine Sergeants watched the Kats for a few minutes then went over to them and corrected their technique, teaching them the basics of Marine hand to hand combat.

Even with the language barrier, slowly the humans and the Kats began to mix and develop a slight bond as the Kats came to understand the humans meant them no harm. Word did leak out that Moshe was upset with this happening, but his own men stood up to him telling him if the humans meant them harm, they would already be dead.

One thing that stood out during this time was if one of the Kats had contact with a female, human or Centaurian, they were about as polite as a Kat could be to prevent a problem such as gotten Peyto killed.

It also did not go unnoticed that Sabrina had all but moved into Carlos's ship when not on duty.

Sabrina stepped out of the refresher, drying herself off from showering after physical training to see Carlos sitting at the small table, sipping on a cup of tea. They had first became loves when Carlos was a Sub-Lieutenant and Sabrina was an Explosives

Specialist during his first cruise. It had been over six years since they had last seen each other, and it seemed as they just picked up where they left off when he was transferred to another ship.

"Sabrina, how is it you never bonded?"

She was drying her mane with the towel when she smiled at him.

"I was married for a time Carlos, but it didn't last."

"Married?"

She laughed.

"Yes, Married. I married an Altairian Xeno-biologist I met during a security detail about a year after you and I parted company."

"What happened? If I'm not prying too much."

"No, it's alright. We were married nearly three years and talked about having children. Can you imagine a Lavender Centaurian? Anyway, we tried without success to conceive. Then one day he asked for a divorce then packed his bags and left. I returned to the Lancers and was promoted last year to Lieutenant."

"Did he tell you why he wanted a divorce?"

"No, but I found out later he moved in with another man, if you understand my meaning."

"I'm sorry Sabrina."

"I'm not. He was a decent lover and a gentleman, but something inside of me always said it would not work out in the long run as hard as I tried to make it work."

"So, what now Sabrina?"

She stepped over to him and gave him a long, passionate kiss, then went to the bed and began getting dressed. Carlos just admired her firm body and smiled knowing the future could get interesting if he just let things happen according to nature.

Arrivals

The arrival of the Federation Diplomatic party was without ceremony. They landed near Carlos's ship and Carlos thought his Aunt had a wicked sense of humor as the lead representative from the Throne was a Centaurian of Denoyelles blood. A distant cousin.

Carlos was standing with Marta next to him with Sabrina on the other side of Marta, separating Marta from Moshe as they watched the elder Centaurian walk towards them. Moshe grunted as he spoke in a low tone.

"You leader sends an old man to treat with my people?"

"Moshe that old man has killed over twenty men in face to face challenges and the Saints only knows how many in open battle against slavers and raiders. Do you wish to see if he is still a great warrior?" Sabrina replied to his comment.

Moshe just growled at Sabrina and she lightly laughed as Carlos stepped forward.

"Lord Pittsburg, it is good to see you again." Carlos spoke as he offered his hand.

"Lord Gannaway, after a certain age, it is good to be seen by anyone." Pittsburg took Carlos's hand then pulled him in and gave him a manly hug which Carlos returned.

"Now Carlos, who do we have here?"

Carlos turned to Marta.

"This is Marta, the Warder of this world and the first person I came in contact with. Marta, Lord Pittsburg."

Pittsburg moved to Marta and offered his hand which she took.

"Lady Marta, it is an honor to meet you. I understand you have a good understanding of our language."

"It is my honor Lord Pittsburg to meet with you. Yes, Lord Carlos has spent hours teaching me your language and how to use his computer to further learn."

"Well Lady Marta, we hope that you can prevent us from making fools of ourselves when we finally meet your peoples representatives."

"Lord Pittsburg, what is this Lady Marta title? I am just Marta."

"Marta, it is a sign, words of respect used by my people. Didn't Carlos explain that to you?"

"No Lord Pittsburg, he did not, but I thank you for the words."

Pittsburg smiled and moved to Sabrina.

"Lieutenant Sativa, it has been some time since we last spoke. How is the family?" He asked as he took her offered hand.

"My parents are well Lord Pittsburg, thank you for asking. Sire, the individual to my left is Moshe, the leader of the band of individuals you probably noticed as you walked up. He is also the individual whom Marta is pledged to be bonded with once these meetings are concluded."

She turned to Moshe.

"Moshe, Lord Pittsburg."

Pittsburg offered his hand which Moshe hesitated in taking. He quickly found out that Pittsburg was stronger than he was as Moshe tried to crush Pittsburg's hand in his grip. Pittsburg just smiled and returned his grip with a greater one until Moshe was able to shake him loose.

"Nice grip Moshe." Pittsburg commented before turning back to Carlos.

"So Carlos, when are the others due to arrive?"

"Five days Demetri."

"Well then, let's see if we can set something up pleasant for the meeting."

"I was thinking a tent, with the sides up to allow for air flow. The climate here is very nice."

"Good idea. Ladies, Moshe, if you will excuse us, we have plans to make."

Pittsburg led Carlos away from the others and once he felt they were far enough away he stopped and turned to Carlos.

"Carlos, Consuela said you were in charge and I have no problem with that arrangement. But try to distance yourself from what has happened since you have been on this world. Any feelings you might have for Marta needs to be put away until this is over. I've read the transcripts of your conversations with your parents and they agree you are too emotionally attached to Marta, even if that emotion is just friendship."

"Demetri, then you know how the men, men like Moshe treat their females."

"Yes Carlos, I know and that is one of the things the Count fought against long ago. This is their world and until we can establish a treaty, bring them into the Federation, we must give way to their manners. Afterwards, the Principles will be taught and things will change for people like Marta, but until then, she is a victim of her own culture."

"She has read the Principles, and has a basic understanding of them. She will become mated to Moshe knowing there is more to the universe than she was raised to believe. Marta will suffer until we can change their thinking and bring equality to their worlds. Demetri, is there anything we can do?"

"No Carlos, not now, not yet. The Principles prevent us from interfering in such matters as much as they prevent such matters once a world enters into the Federation. This is a new race; a new species of humanity and we have to tread carefully."

"I understand Demetri. But for the record, there is nothing between Marta and myself except a sense of friendship after a rocky first meeting. I do feel responsible for her since I placed her in the position to learn about the universe we live in."

Pittsburg placed his hand on Carlos's shoulder before he responded.

"Carlos, you are so very much like your father. It's what made him a great leader. Do not loose focus on the end results which will eventually grant your wishes for Marta. Until then put her aside and continue to march."

Carlos just nodded his head then they walked to an area away from the shuttles and Assault Boats as a place to set up the meeting tent. Even during the discussions on how to set up the meeting, Demetri noticed that Carlos seemed distracted.

"Okay Carlos, what is on your mind?"

"I've given some thought about this being a new species and their culture. Do we have a right to interfere, even if we find it goes against all we have been raised to believe?"

"Carlos, we know nothing about this race and to be honest, I have debated that same question for decades. The Count first changed a world system then the universe with his rules, making each person, regardless of sex or race equal in the eyes of humanity. Even though I am not in direct line of the Denoyelles family, I too am burdened with the curse of having to defend the

Principles of Leadership when there has been times I think an exception should be made."

"Because of the blood that flows through our veins, we are cursed to attend to the Principles and protect humanity from the evils of the universe. Having said that, once again, this is a new species of humanity and until we know more about them, learn of their past, can we attempt to adjust their future as members of the Federation."

"You're a wise man Demetri. Now I know why Aunt Consuela sent you to watch over me during these times. Course, you being a Centaurian does help matters considering your physical appearance and our new friends."

"After meeting Moshe, I would be hard pressed to call them friends just yet. I understand his men have somewhat rebelled against him and have been developing friendships with the Marines and Lancers. Depending on Moshe's political power, this could be a problem during the initial discussions. Unless Moshe directly challenges you, ignore him as best you can and do not provoke him for any reason. Understood?"

"Understood Demetri."

The next fives days were taken up with setting the tent and arrangements for the meeting. When the Kats learned that the tent being set up was for meeting their delegation, three of them helped under the guidance of the Marines doing the work. There was still a low level of tension between the humans and the Kats, but the Marines having long experience in dealing with hostile people found ways to lighten things up when possible.

The Kats were also invaluable in helping Carlos determine seating. A standard chair could be uncomfortable for the Kat's tails so Carlos had bench like seating made for all including the human attendees so all would have the same seating.

The Meeting

The ship carrying the Kat's delegation landed near Moshe's ship with Moshe and crew present to greet the delegation as they exited the ship. All of the shuttles and Assault Boats had shifted locations with three Assault Boats in the air with their gunners watching over the action on the ground.

There was an Honor Guard made up of Marines leading into the tent which Carlos had spent some time explaining to Moshe the meaning of it so he could inform the delegation upon their arrival. Marta was not allowed to join the Kat's who were greeting the delegation since she was a female, but Carlos had her standing between Demetri and himself as they waited near the tent.

The first individual off the ship surprised Carlos and company as the individual was not a Kat. He did not walk down the ramp as he lumbered down it. He was huge in form as the only way he could be described. His fur was a dark brown and he resembled a bear. Demetri leaned over and whispered to Carlos.

"Ursine Major?"

"It would seem so, and look what's following."

The second individual was covered in nearly coal black fur and even though smaller than the first, he was still large in size.

"Carlos, I wonder if this is where the tale of the werewolf comes from?"

"This is impossible Demetri, yet we are seeing it with our own eyes. There is more to these people than we know and may ever learn."

They watched as Moshe met the new people, bowing deeply to them. As Moshe spoke to the new arrivals, from time to time they would look in the direction of the tent and the humans gathered there. Marta had stood quietly between the men as they exchanged comments to each other.

Soon the new people dismissed Moshe and walked towards the tent with the Honor Guard presenting arms as they passed them. They stopped about four meters from Carlos and company. Before Carlos or Demetri could speak, the bear like creature spoke.

"I am Tamas, speaker for the Council. This is Mewa, who will treat with you humans for the Council."

"I am Carlos Gannaway, human discoverer of this world and appointed by the Federation Throne to treat with your people. This is Marta, warder of this world…"

Tamas raised his paw like hand and spoke.

"This female has no value in our talks. She is to return to our world and bond with Moshe."

"Tamas, she has a great understanding on our language and I would like her to be present to translate between us so there can be no misunderstanding."

"I understand your language well. I have learned your language from one of your devils that came to steal and violate our females."

Demetri spoke up before Carlos could answer.

"Lord Tamas, I am Demetri, second to Carlos in these talks. The one called Marta could be of great service to you and Mewa in these talks."

Mewa spoke in their language which Tamas translated.

"Mewa is tired of this talk concerning the female. He wants to know why the one called Carlos attacked Moshe when he landed to take the female home then allowed one of the females we have noticed here to kill one of his men."

"Moshe lies, deceives Mewa. Moshe attacked me before I could even greet him. His man Peyto was killed by one of the females in a challenge when he violated the terms of the contest and the female killed him which by our world's traditions was fair and right."

Tamas spoke to Mewa who replied back to him.

"It is your word against Moshe who is a great warrior."

"Mewa, I can prove Moshe is lying. And he is not a great warrior as I challenged him and he tucked his tail and walked away."

Tamas's eyes grew big then spoke the words to Mewa. As he was doing that, Carlos whispered to Marta.

"Is he properly translating my words."

"Yes, Lord Carlos, he is." Her head was turned down, not looking at anyone.

Tamas turned back to Carlos.

"You say you can prove your claims against Moshe. How is this so?"

"Everything that occurs outside the ships is recorded to insure we do not violate our own laws. We are not like the ones who came before us, we wish to treat with your people, to join with them in peace."

"You wish to join with us in peace yet you have warships in space above us, and warriors on the soil. You do this to force us to accept you into our gatherings. How can we believe what you say to us?"

Demetri turned back to one of the female Centaurians that was lined up behind them and she handed him a holo-pad which Demetri placed on the ground between himself and Tamas. He keyed the remote he took from his pocket and from the holo-pad rose the image of Moshe leaving his ship that first day and walking towards Carlos and Marta. Tamas stepped back from the holo-pad as he and Mewa watched events unfold. The image was unaltered and the audio was clear. When Carlos disappeared, Tamas jumped back and Mewa growled as they watched Moshe's staff explode then Carlos reappear with his Katana in his hand.

Even though Carlos and the other humans could not understand what Marta was saying to Moshe before he struck her, Tamas and Mewa could. Demetri stopped the replay just before Carlos moved to help Marta up.

Mewa spoke but it was not Tamas who replied, but Marta. She spoke in her native language then just remained quiet until Carlos asked what was said.

"Lord Carlos, Mewa asked if what he just watched was true and not something made up for their viewing. I said it was true."

Carlos turned back to Tamas.

"Would Mewa like to see the record of the challenge between Peyto and our female called Karina?"

Tamas translated and Mewa thought for a moment, looking down at the Holo-pad before answering. Tamas translated.

"Mewa says that if the challenge was violated by Peyto and the female killed Peyto in response to that violation, then he has no concern about Peyto's death. Nothing more will be spoken about that challenge."

"Thank You Mewa." Carlos replied.

Mewa then spoke to Marta who responded then Mewa spoke again. Marta turned to Carlos.

"Lord Carlos, I am ordered to go with Moshe back to our world and accept my bonding with him. I have no choice in this matter as it is a point of my family's honor. I must go and gather my things and we shall leave once I am aboard Moshe's ship."

"Marta, I wish I could stop this from happening but I must abide by your culture in these matters. If I never see you again, please know that I am grateful for your friendship and the time we had together."

Carlos reached down and took her hands, brought them up and gently kissed them before letting her go. He turned to Tamas as she walked away.

"Tamas, please advise Mewa that I kissed Marta's hands as a sign of friendship, and her honor is pure."

Tamas translated to Mewa who just nodded his head in response.

As Marta returned to her habitat, Carlos indicated for all to enter the tent and sit as they talked about the future. In less than ten minutes, Marta exited her habitat with a simple shoulder bag and walked to Moshe's ship without looking towards the tent and Carlos.

Sabrina met Marta before she could enter the ship and spoke to her then kissed both her cheeks. The last Carlos saw of Marta as she entered the ship. The ships engines were coming up to power as the ramp drew up and the hatch closed on the ship.

Via the earbud Carlos was wearing, he heard Sabrina advise the Destroyer Dauntless that Moshe's ship was lifting as per orders from the senior alien on the planet. Carlos closed his mind of Marta and focused on the talks allowing Demetri to handle the negotiations.

As the talks were proceeding at a snails pace, the Marines had gone hunting and once more began cooking half an animal over an open pit. Demetri had to explain that this was their way of greeting who they hoped would one day be good friends and allies in the hunt for the kind of people that had raided and killed many of their people.

Carlos had to explain why he had come to this world and his purpose for coming. He carefully worded his explanation so Tamas could grasp the meaning of his words and in the back of his mind, he knew that Marta could have expressed those feelings as they had talked for hours as they waited for Moshe to arrive.

The day ended with everyone eating around the meeting table with Mewa complimenting on how the meat was prepared. When Carlos introduced Karna, the female Centaurian who had overseen the cooking of the meat, Mewa was hesitant in meeting her but found a way to compliment her without sounding as if he was insulted by speaking to a female.

The talks lasted for four days with Tamas and Mewa slowly adjusting to the fact the females with Carlos were not only treated as equals, they were armed to the teeth. On the morning of the third day, Sabrina and Karina put on a sword fighting display using training swords against each other, then a display of the strength and sharpness of their blades against various objects starting with melons they gathered from the planet's surface to the leg of a cow taken for eating with the meat still attached.

The Marines put on a firepower display utilizing only a half section of troopers, then a display of hand to hand techniques, only showing some of the basics so as not to give away too many secrets to the aliens. But it was the short, but violent display of firepower that the Marines' Assault Boats put on that convinced Mewa to sit down and make plans for further meetings.

It was quickly discovered that the aliens manner of keeping time was different from the Federations, so Carlos had the Chief Engineer aboard the Destroyer Dauntless construct a clock, a timer which counted down days via the Federation manner of tracking time and days and it was presented to Mewa as a way to know when they were to meet again.

They were told that when the clock reached zero, it would send a signal for them to come and guide them to their home world. But if the Council decides not to meet with them, they only had to place the clock in water and the water would cause the clock to stop working along with the signal generator. But inside the clock was a coded tracking device like those used in escape pods so once taken back to the alien's home world, Carlos would know where that planet was located for future reference.

During the final session, it was discovered that the planet they were on was basically one of the aliens farm planets, where they harvested meats for their home world. Once a year, or annual, ships arrived to harvest parts of the herds of animals on the planet for the larders of the home world.

The next meeting was set to correspond with the next harvest and the aliens wanted the Federation people off the planet when it happened. Carlos once more had to explain his reason for being on the planet, and now his purpose for staying on the planet so that if they wished to further discuss aspects of meeting with the Federation, he would be available to them since they did not have any other manner of communications between the two peoples.

When Carlos explained how the minerals, the riches of the planet he had discovered could be removed from the planet, Mewa loudly protested. Until a treaty could be arranged, there would be no ripping of the soil to get at the treasures which rightfully belong to his people even though the aliens had no knowledge or usage for some of those minerals.

Carlos took advantage of their lack of knowledge and proposed that he would continue to survey the planet, and would only take that which was laying above the soil, and he demonstrated that concept by picking up a stone lying near the tent. Mewa, not knowing what Carlos knew gave him permission to pick up anything he wanted as long as he did not harm the surface of the planet.

With the meetings being recorded, and Mewa giving permission for Carlos to prospect the surface of the planet, Carlos just side stepped several Federation regulations giving him one hundred percent of the profit of anything he retrieved and sold.

After the aliens returned to their ship for the evening, Demetri asked Carlos about that prospection agreement.

"Carlos, if I remember the articles on prospecting, Mewa not only gave you free reign on this world, but now you no longer have to split the money from anything you find with the Federation."

"Correct Demetri, I'm surprised you are aware of that obscure paragraph in the articles."

"The way you have been hedging on that with Mewa, I reread the articles last night and you're right, it is a very obscure point in them. It makes one wonder how it got into the articles."

"According to the history of those articles, it was put in because there was some protest that if the owner of a world gave permission, than the Federation had no control over the situation. It was never considered that a prospector would discover a rich world owned by an alien race who just might allow such prospecting."

"Let me ask you this Carlos, just how wealthy did you become when Mewa gave you that authorization to surface mine this world?"

"Demetri my friend, how would you like to have your own, personal Destroyer to travel about in?"

"Are you serious?"

"Yes, but now the catch is I have to do all the labor to gain those riches. But it will give me something to do as we wait for the clock to wind down until we meet with them again. Granted maybe it was wrong of me to take advantage of these people, but they set the standards, and I just used them to my own benefit. On the other side of that coin, if we do finalize a treaty with these people, I'll make sure they also benefit from this adventure."

Sabrina came to them after making her evening rounds of her people and sat down beside Carlos as he and Demetri were having that discussion. Carlos sat for a minute then excused himself, going into his ship. When he returned, he had a ball of cloth in his hand which he handed to Sabrina.

"Open it Sabrina."

She unwrapped the object and just held it out in her hands for a minute before commenting.

"Carlos, is this a diamond?"

"Yes, and it is pure according to my readings, and weights just under two kilos."

"And you found that on top of the soil?" Demetri inquired.

"Yes, and it's not the largest I found. I only need a way to lift what I can gather to this location. The aircar will lift two metric tons in a sling load, and I just need containers to place the diamonds into for such movement. And this is not the only item which I can harvest. I am going to be very busy for a long time."

Sabrina wrapped the diamond back up and handed it back to Carlos. That night after they had showered and made love, he told Sabrina to take the diamond with her when she left so she would have something put away for when she left the Lancers. She sat up in bed and looked at him.

"Carlos, I'm not a prostitute you have to pay for my time in your bed."

"Sabrina, I didn't mean it that way and you should know better than to make such a comment."

"I'm sorry Carlos, you're right. I didn't come to your bed because of the wealth you have access too, I came here because of you, who you really are inside."

"I don't know who I am inside anymore, but I hope it is someone to be proud of knowing."

Sabrina leaned over and kissed him.

"Rich or poor you are a man amongst men. Even after I married, I often thought about you and how tender you are and giving to your lover. Maybe that was wrong of me, but you left a mark on me that will never go away."

Neither spoke again as she laid down resting her head on his shoulder then later rolling off him and going to sleep.

Carlos lay in the subdued light of his ship thinking he should marry her, but considered that he could very easily leave her a widow with this adventure.

He knew he had shamed Moshe and figured if the situation presented itself, Moshe would either kill him or have him killed to wipe the shame from his being. And there was nothing the Fleet could do to stop one of the alien ships from returning to this world.

A week later the Lancers were ordered off the planet for another mission along the rim of known space. Sabrina had a box made for the diamond and it was sealed, preventing prying eyes from looking into it. She sent it to her parents on Zyra for safe keeping until she ended her time as a Lancer.

Their last night together was passionate before she said her goodbyes to him and lifted to the Lancer Assault Carrier she was posted too.

Picking Up Rocks

After a long discussion with his father and aunt, Carlos contacted the Fleet's Replenishment/Supply ship that was supporting the coverage of the alien worlds and requested the empty transfer cases they always had on board.

The cases were lightweight yet more than durable to load the items Carlos was going to gather from the planet's surface. They were designed to be sling loaded if necessary with eyelets at each corner and moved by aircar. They also had lids that could be code locked to prevent pilfering while on a planet's surface.

Carlos first went to where the crystals were locate and unless he had to dig one out, he pulled them from the surface. By not digging a crystal out, he kept with the intent of the agreement, but disturbing the soil by pulling a crystal from the ground was not digging or ripping into the soil. Within a week, he had filled one container with crystals and sealed it for transport to Hollis, where his parents lived.

He next went to the diamond field and he barely half filled a container before abandoning the area. The open vein of platinum was easier that he thought to harvest as it pulled out of the side of the bluff with ease. From there he cut the ribbon of metal with a vibra-saw into pieces that would fit into a container. He only filled about a fourth of the container before he moved on to the area with gold in it.

Carlos spent his days clearing out the areas he had surveyed then went in search of other areas to harvest. It did not matter to him what the mineral was, if it was above ground, he harvested it. He had moved away from Marta's habitat, establishing a camp further up in the hills where the bulk of the riches of this world could be found.

Seven weeks into his search for riches, a freighter arrived to transport his containers to Hollis for determination of value and sale by an employee of the family who dealt in minerals. The freighter also brought additional containers in case Carlos needed more. The freighter was in orbit for five weeks until Carlos determined he had worked this continent to its limit.

Carlos moved to the next continent and started all over again gathering minerals. There were days it was almost back breaking work, bending over to gather the items he had came in search for, but he was driven by the knowledge he had done this all himself, not by allowing others to do the work for him.

On the second continent, he had to work around the herds of animals to harvest what he could. Here he found a lake which the herds drank from that according to the sensors was littered with diamonds below the surface of the lake.

The Destroyer Dauntless had been replaced by the Destroyer Medford and he contacted it to arrange rebreathing apparatus and dive equipment to check out the lake. The Medford sent down a Dive NCO to insure he was certified to use the equipment plus to act as a Safety diver in case of trouble.

The process of gathering the diamonds became simple when the Dive NCO suggested Carlos gather up and fill a mesh bag, then tie that bag to a buoy maker, then move on to fill the next bag. A boat was brought down with motor so they could move about the lake without having to constantly returning to the shore.

It took two weeks to basically farm the lake with Carlos filling a shipping container. The Marine Senior Sergeant left the surface with a sealed box containing rough diamonds worth more than twenty years of service could have paid him.

The next continent was not as well supplied with what Carlos could harvest but he did fill one container with crystals before he finally decided he had enough based upon his rough calculations of the value of what he had lifted to the freighter.

There was nothing more for Carlos to do except return to Marta's habitat and wait for the clock to wind down and prepare for the next meeting with the aliens. This gave him too much time to think, to ponder the events of the past months and how his life had changed.

He came to recognize he was in fact in love with Marta, but not as a lover, but as if she was a younger sister. He had pushed her into learning things she would never have known if not for him and he carried a guilt of knowing her life would not be as she had once dreamed it would be before his landing on this world. Carlos had inadvertently taken an innocent and corrupted her view of life by showing her how life was away from her closed universe.

Carlos also came to realize that he was in love with Sabrina and probably had been so from the first time they were together. Certainly he had other lovers over the years but none fill his soul as she did when they were together. She had admitted much of the same about him even when she was married to another. But Carlos was actually afraid to ask her to marry him considering the chances he was now taking and the risk she had spoken of concerning Moshe.

When the Medford notified Carlos there were two alien ships entering the system, Carlos lifted to avoid any contact with the aliens who were coming to harvest meat for their larders. He had tied the aircar to the top of his ship and insured he left nothing except a few empty crates on the planet's surface.

He took a stationary orbit near the Medford as added protection against any attempt on his life. The Medford invited him to dock with them and utilize their facilities but Carlos was polite in declining the offer. He also knew that there was a former lover aboard that ship who he would rather not see at this time.

Carlos received a report on the DNA of Marta and the others including Tamas and Mewa that they had been able to collect. These were humans that had been genetically modified to

80

their current forms. Once the mutated genetic markers had been removed, the DNA's taken showed they had originated on Old Earth including the animal forms which they had been blended with.

This was not an experiment done by Hayutans similar that which led to the rise of the Centaurians, but by another unknown race, but for what purpose was unknown.

Carlos felt trapped in a prison of his own making. He had initiated contact with a new race while at the same time was mining the planet he had discovered. His claim to the planet was valid and the authorization to basically surface mine it was valid to include the Thrones agreement that he did have the right under the articles of exploration and prospecting, so he was not concerned about a claim jumper especially since there was a Fleet standing guard, preventing any other humans from encroaching upon these worlds.

It would take at least two months for his cargo to reach Hollis by freighter and then at least a month before he knew where he stood as far as any wealth he had earned. His desire to be separate from the family, the Denoyelles Clan had suddenly placed him in the forefront of the family, and having to live up to the Principles of Leadership which were ingrained into each member of the Clan.

With the weight of his aunt sitting on the Throne and his father one of the great heroes of the Federation, he now had to live up to their reputations even though both would tell him to just be himself.

Carlos felt there was a curse on the family going all the way back to the Count himself, but first came to light when Prince Michael discovered the inhabitants of Bellus and married the last Princess of Bellus, Kaya. It seemed whenever a people needed help, needed to discover their own place in the universe, a member of the Denoyelles Clan found themselves in the middle of it all, regardless how far from Count Conrad Denoyelles they were in the genetic family tree.

The Denoyelles Family was the wealthiest family in the universe and that came from hard work and finding managers who would take care of their businesses without having to look over their shoulders. The trust fund that Carlos inherited upon leaving the Fleet would have provided for him the rest of his life without every having to lift a finger, but he was driven to prove himself, to prove to the universe that just because he had Denoyelles blood in his veins, he could make something of himself without the trust fund.

But he often had to laugh at that idea since he had used the money from the trust fund to buy and transform the ship he was using and pay for the things he needed to separate himself from the family.

Carlos returned to the planet once the aliens had left and just wandered the planet without a goal in sight as he waited for the meeting clock to wind down and Demetri to return with others to meet with the aliens.

When Demetri returned, he had with him a select group of Federation personal who were more noted as being warriors as diplomats, and they were selected from various races within the Federation so the aliens would see the diversity of the Federation.

Carlos joined them on the Heavy Cruiser Creedmoor for the trip to the aliens home world. He was apprehensive as he wondered how he would feel once he saw Marta again if that was possible.

A Painful Reunion

Carlos made the trip to the home world without any attachments even though he could have enjoyed a playmate nightly. This was one problem being who he was and his ancestors had written about it in their journals. Being from such a wealthy and powerful family brought females to his bed with many in hopes of finding a permanent arrangement within the family.

He remembered the first time he took Sabrina to his bed. It was only after he had failed several times and she made it clear she was only there to enjoy the sex, but for him to forget about anything other than that. That one night lasted for nearly five months.

On the second night of the voyage, he was surprised by Vanna and Karina being aboard along with Ayesha and Jeniree, two other Centaurian Lancer females. Their purpose was to execute a plan which came directly from the Throne, and that was to find Marta and check on her safety.

A micro-tracking device had been placed on her shoulder bag when Sabrina stopped and talked to her before Marta boarded Moshe's ship. Using cloaking devices, the four female Lancer's were going to find Marta and check on her, then report her condition back to Carlos. Carlos never understood why the Throne was interested in Marta's safety, but just accepted the Lancer's orders and put it aside.

Carlos asked where Sabrina was and was told she was on another assignment. Karina indicated she was available to share his bed, but he was polite in turning her offer down.

The Cruiser only took five days to travel to the alien's home world with their greatly improve engines over what the aliens had at their disposal. Along with the Cruiser were four cloaked Scout ships that were along in case the delegation needed a quick escape from the planet. There was also a full company of

Marines with cloaked Assault Boats that would be standing by if needed.

Each member of the delegation would wear cloaking devices along with weapons that could not be detected by metal detectors if the aliens had knowledge and use of such devices.

Princess Consuela issued final instructions to the delegation to work towards a peaceful settlement between the Federation and this new race of people, but to take no chances with their own safety.

The landing site was indicated by the signal from the clock on what appeared to be their main spaceport. The first humans off the shuttle were two Marines who positioned themselves at the foot of the ramp and just stood, watching the area as Carlos followed by Demetri and the others exited the shuttle. The only individual to meet them was Tamas with a group of Kat's standing behind him.

Tamas reacted to the Marines at the ramp.

"Lord Carlos, what are those armed men doing here?" He pointed at the Marines.

"Tamas, they are there to insure no one enters our shuttle and causes a problem which might cause myself and the delegation harm."

"No person would do such a thing. Remove them."

"Tamas, if I remove them and something happens to the shuttle, the Federation Fleet will come and lay waste to your world. We come in peace and even on our worlds, Marines stand watch on our shuttles and ships. They will stay."

Tamas seemed confused until he had a chance to digest what Carlos had said then he turned to the Kats behind him and barked orders to them. The Kats scrambled to surround the shuttle as if to protect it from attackers.

Carlos put his glasses on and watched as Vanna and company exited the shuttle, slipped between the Kats and moved off in the direction of the signal they were receiving.

"Shall we go Tamas?" Carlos put to Tamas.

The transportation to the Council chambers was in a vehicle which would be considered an antique on Federation worlds. Everyone noticed the engine was fueled by petroleum and it was in need of maintenance.

As noticed from space, the city had no specific design of streets or buildings which were mostly single level structures made of wood and stone. They stopped at a large, single story building away from the center of the city and escorted in a large room with a table and a mixture of individuals waiting for them. A mixture was all that Carlos could describe to himself as it seemed he had walked into a masquerade party were everyone was costumed as their favorite animal.

Tamas introduced Carlos and company to each before they sat at the table with an older Wolf like individual with grey fur as the leader of the people. He immediately complained about the Fleet standing off outside their share of the universe and once more Carlos had to explain through Tamas they purpose.

The first two hours were dealt with explaining once more the whole purpose of their being there and what brought them to the worlds these people utilized. When it came to the clock, the leader, Bellu, said they did not feel it was right to be forced into this meeting by outsiders. Carlos once more explained that they could have destroyed the clock, but that was just brushed off with a wave of the hand.

Three hours later the meeting adjourned and Carlos and company returned to the Creedmoor until the next day. Vanna reported they had located the abode where Marta's tracking device was sending from, but had yet to see anyone except Moshe and one of his wives outside the house at that time.

The second day was no better as the delegation was questioned about the Federation and how people lived, then attempted to degrade the quality of life that members of the Federation lived with on a day to day basis. The proclaimed they had an idyllic world yet the survey's from the Scout Ships showed very little agriculture or animal life to provide for the population of the planet.

But when Carlos mentioned the ancient ruins in the Northern Polar region, the meeting came to a sudden halt with their leader, Bellu proclaiming there were no ruins on the planet, only peaceful towns. Carlos tried to explain through Tamas what ruins were, but even Tamas refused to cooperate and the room emptied, leaving the Federation delegation alone.

It was during the landing approach of the shuttle to the Creedmoor that Vanna contacted Carlos.

"Carlo, this is Vanna, how do you read, over?"

"Go ahead Vanna, over."

"We think we've ID'd Marta, but the view is obscure, and it seems she has changed, over."

"Vanna, explain changed, over."

"She seems listless, out of focus, and it looks as if her tail has been removed, over."

There was a long pause before Carlos responded.

"Vanna, have you seen tails on his other wives, over?"

"Affirmative Carlos, over."

"Vanna, I'll contact you once I am back aboard the Creedmoor to give you further instructions, over."

"Understand, out."

Once in his quarters, Carlos contacted Vanna with a video link with Demetri and Doctor Bradford, the Altairian doctor assigned to the delegation.

"Vanna, can you get a closer look at the subject, over?"

"Standby, connecting you to Ayesha who has moved closer, over."

A few minutes later, the video split and showed what Ayesha was seeing. The subject's hair or mane had been almost shaved, her tail had been removed and her face looked as if it was scarred now. The subject was wearing a course smock that was either a light brown or was filthy from its appearance at this distance. The subject just sat on the bench with her hands hanging and her head down looking at the ground.

"Vanna, if you can, get in and take a DNA sample of the subject and see if we have a match, over."

"Roger Carlos, and if we have a match, over?"

"If possible, pull her out of that environment during the night, over."

"Understand, perform a snatch. We'll get back with you when we have more information, over."

"Be careful Vanna, Carlos out."

Carlos was awaken from a restless sleep by his communicator beeping. He checked his chronometer to find it was 0417 hours in the morning. He answered the call.

"Carlos here."

"This is Vanna, we have Marta and DNA confirms identity. She was locked in a room by herself sleeping on the floor and the other wives had beds in a common room, over."

"What else Vanna, over?"

"Carlos, it is best you see for yourself. Jeniree juiced her before we left with her to make sure she did not cause us any problems. She is pregnant, over."

Carlos just sat and considered how to deal with this situation as his anger grew. He knew he had to calm down before he ruined everything they were trying to accomplish.

"Vanna, have her at the meeting site at 0800 and stay cloaked. Be ready to follow us into the building and the meeting room, over."

"Understand Carlos. If I may, keep your feelings contained because you are not going to like what you see, over."

"Thank you Vanna, out."

Carlos showered then dressed before seeking out the Marine Commander on the ship. He instructed the Marines to be ready to drop on his orders once the delegation leaves the ship. After he had that arranged, he went to one of the Scout ships that had docked with the Creedmoor and instructed them to go down to the planet and if the individual named Moshe attempted to run, leave the planet, to take him into custody being cautious of his claws. The Scout ship detached and went to the surface to watch Moshe's abode.

Just as the delegation was preparing to drop to the planet, Carlos received a message that Moshe had left the house with a shoulder bag and was heading in the direction of the space port. Carlos just smiled thinking that the Scouts would take him at the space port where they had plenty room to land.

Since they were dropping nearly an hour early, Carlos told the shuttle pilot to put them down in front of the meeting building. This caused a bit of a stir amongst the inhabitants when they landed and the shuttle just sat on the ground without taking back off. Carlos saw Vanna and company standing out of the way of foot traffic and the shuttle with Marta being held up between them. They were still cloaked but his glasses told him this was not going to be a pleasant reunion between him and Marta. He just motioned for them to follow, mixed in with the delegation.

Once inside the meeting room, Marta was placed on a stool and Jeniree positioned herself to assist her in sitting up. Carlos kneeled in front of her, lifting her head up so he could look at her. She had scars on both sides of her face from claws being raked across her face. Had she done this to herself, or had Moshe? Her tail was missing and her clothing was filthy.

"Marta, can you hear me? It's Carlos. I've came to see that you are alright."

She just looked at him with dead eyes. Carlos motioned to Doctor Bradford to attend to her. Bradford had an advance version of the Pocket Doc and began scanning her. He checked down her body as she just sat until he had what readings he needed before addressing Carlos.

"Carlos, she has some substance in her system that has her zombied out. It's not in my drug reference and without putting her into a hospital, no way to know what it is or how to counter it. But even without the drug she cannot answer you. Her tongue has been removed."

Carlos could barely contain his anger upon hearing about her condition. He felt he had caused this and he would make Moshe pay for his cruelty. He kneeled in front of her and took her hands in his and felt something wrong. Looking at her hand the tips of her fingers were scarred telling him her claws had been removed, probably by jerking them out. He had Bradford check her fingers and he confirmed her claws were missing.

A few minutes later, Tamas arrived with a group of armed Kats and demanded why they had arrived early and landed in front of the building. When he saw Marta, he demanded she be removed from the building as only the males could come into the Council building.

When Carlos stood, Tamas noticed he was armed, then he looked at the others to see they were also armed with swords and handguns. Tamas started to panic and back out of the room when his guards began falling to the floor as Vanna's team began shooting them with Electro-darts from their cloaked positions. Soon Tamas was standing alone as members of the delegation began dragging the unconscious bodies into the meeting chamber.

The eight guards were tied up with gags on their mouths and lined up along a wall, sitting up with all their weapons removed and in the corner near the entry to the room. Carlos looked at Tamas with a grin that scared him.

"Tamas, sit down and stay quiet and you might live to tell you grandchildren about this day."

As Tamas sat down he took another look at Marta before speaking.

"Who is this female you have brought into these chambers?"

"This is Marta, and she is now under my protection. Soon Moshe will be captured and brought here to answer for his crimes against her."

Tamas started to speak then decided to stay quiet.

Over the next half hour the alien delegates arrived and each complained about a female in their chambers, then about the human delegation being armed, but it seemed an unknown source was preventing them from leaving. That unknown, unseen source was Vanna and her team pushing them back with the butts of their carbines.

As this was happening, Moshe entered the space port and began running towards his ship knowing he had to get off the planet before the one called Carlos came hunting for him. He awoke to the calls from one of his wives telling him that Marta was missing but what panicked him was the uniform badge pinned to the door to Marta's room. It was the badge of a Lancer that he remembered from his contact with them on the farm world.

He was running as fast as he could and ran headlong into the cloaked Scout ship, knocking himself out. Three cloaked gunners from the ship exited, covered his hands and bound his wrists behind him before carrying him into the ship.

"Carlos, this is Scout ship Bengie, we have Moshe, over."

Carlos smiled as the news of Moshe's capture came through the headset he was wearing.

"Bengie, uncloak and bring him to me. Vanna will guide you into the building, out."

Vanna slipped out the open door to meet with the Scouts when they landed. Ten minutes later, the Scout ship could be heard landing in from of the Council building. Moshe was carried into the meeting room still unconscious and a gash on his forehead from running into the side of the Scout ship.

Moshe was deposited on the table of the meeting room, then the Scouts just stood back, ready for a fight if one started. Bellu became very vocal at the intrusion of armed men and how Moshe was being treated. Carlos laughed and told him to be quiet, then told Jeniree to uncloak and treat Moshe's head injury before waking him up.

When Jeniree decloaked, it was almost a panic in the room, but the Council knew they had no way out of the room without injury, even death from these invaders.

With her helmet on along with her uniform and equipment, there was no way to determine if Jeniree was male or female. She treated Moshe's wound, sealing it and cleaning his blood from his face before injecting him with a potent drug to wake him up.

Moshe slowly awoke and once conscious enough to understand his situation, he became panicked and began yelling as he struggled to get up. Carlos moved to the edge of the table and Moshe tried to roll off the other side when he saw him, remembering what Carlos had told him back on the other planet.

Carlos grabbed Moshe by the mane and jerked him back to his side of the table as he spoke to him.

"Moshe, you remember what I told you about harming Marta, don't you?"

Moshe's eyes got big and he began talking in his own language. Carlos slapped him and told him to be quiet, then turned to Tamas.

"What did he say Tamas?"

Tamas was as frightened as the other creatures in the room and stammered out the translation.

"He was calling for the Council to help him."

Carlos once more laughed.

"Moshe there is no help for you. But you will tell me why Marta is as she sits here today. Why you did the things to her that destroyed a beautiful person and mind. You will tell me or I will remove parts of your body until you talk to me."

Moshe struggled against his restraints only to find he was trapped and had no place to escape too.

"Moshe, why did you remove her tongue so she could not speak?"

"She was speaking heresy to the others, telling them it was my seed that gave me female off spring. She was teaching them your tongue so they could speak to you humans when you came."

"Moshe it is your seed that determines if the child is male or female, just as my seed makes that same determination in my people. You are a fool Moshe. Why did you cut off her tail?"

"When she learned she was with child, she used her tail to prevent me from mating with her. Covering her parts with her tail so I could not enter her."

"So you violated her when she did not want you too, after she knew she was with your child? And her hair? Her mane?"

"I cut it off and sent it to her family as a sign of disgrace."

Carlos stepped back from Moshe and as tempting as it was to pull his sword and remove his head right there, he had another thought.

"Take this garbage out into the street, strip him from the waist up and insure he has no weapons on him. Moshe, I challenged you once before and you turned tail. Today fight me or die a coward. Take him outside. Tamas, tell the Council they will also go outside and observe what happens."

As Tamas was moving the Council out of the room behind Moshe and the Scouts, Demetri moved over to Carlos.

"Carlos is this wise? He is still part feline and they do have good reflexes plus his claws."

"Demetri, if he fights like Peyto, the one Karina killed, I have a better than even chance even if I do get clawed a few times. All through these talks they have held they are superior than we humans. Moshe is supposed to be one of their great warriors, so I think it is time to show them otherwise. Remember they were fighting raiders, slavers, not someone like you or I. Besides, I owe

Marta because I put her in a bad situation by exposing her to our world through the computer."

"You get yourself killed out there and her Highness just might skin me alive."

Carlos laughed and patted Demetri on the shoulder then turned and left the room with the others following. Moshe was in the middle of the street being stripped and searched as Carlos walked over to the shuttle ramp and began removing his weapons, placing them on the ramp.

"Carlos, he is clean."

He turned towards Vanna's voice but because he had taken his glasses off, he could not see her.

"Vanna, you and Jeniree uncloak, leave the others cloaked and standby."

Vanna uncloaked and moved aside as Carlos continued to strip in the same manner as Moshe. Vanna ducked inside the shuttle and returned with a pair of clear, wrap-around glasses and handed them to Carlos.

"Protect your eyes from his claws."

"Good idea, thanks. Now say a small prayer to the Saints I have not bitten off more than I can chew."

Carlos took a deep breath, then moved to face Moshe.

"Remove his restraints." Carlos ordered.

He waited until Moshe was free to fight before speaking to him.

"Now Moshe you have a choice, fight me or die on your knees as I take your head. If you win, you go free."

The days and weeks of prospecting, lifting and carrying the weights of the minerals he had been collecting had caused Carlos to bulk up, muscle up even more than he was before landing on the planet.

Moshe looked around and knew he had no other choice than fight Carlos but he had his claws where this human only had his hands. Moshe dropped to a crouch, ready to pounce as he moved closer to Carlos who just stood facing him. A large crowd of people were gathering around to watch this combat between a human and the one they saw as their great warrior.

As Moshe slowly began to circle Carlos, Carlos kept pace with him, turning with him, just allowing his feet to shift without tangling himself up, ready to counter any attack Moshe might make.

Moshe lunged at Carlos with his claws extended and tried to get a grip on Carlos, but Carlos just knocked his hands out of the way and as Moshe's lunge took him past Carlos, Carlos hit him with a downward backfist to the side of Moshe's head, nearly dropping him to his knees.

This set the stage for the attacks by Moshe on Carlos as he continued to try to get a grip on Carlos, but Carlos would block the attack and strike him where ever he found an opening. Carlos was wearing on Moshe's body with blocks and strikes to head, neck and torso while suffering two claw marks across his chest that were slowly seeping blood.

Finally Carlos unleashed a series of kicks and strikes with his fists that staggered Moshe back until he fell down on his face. Carlos dropped onto Moshe's back with a knee, knocking the air from his lungs, then wrapped his arm around Moshe's neck, choking him as Moshe tried to get his claws into Carlos. Moshe did manage to dig his claws into Carlos's arm around his neck but it did no good as Carlos was starving him of oxygen until Moshe collapsed, unconscious.

Carlos held his choke hold a few more seconds then released him, and stood up over his body. He looked down on Moshe for a moment then stepped away with Jeniree moving to him to provide first aid to the claw marks on his chest and arm. He stopped her before she could attend to him.

"Check on him, see if he is still alive."

Jeniree moved to Moshe, checked for a pulse on his neck then rolled him over and checked the reactions of his eyes even if those eyes were more animal than human.

"He lives Carlos."

Carlos looked around at the people watching the fight before speaking.

"Someone hold him down, spread eagle so he cannot move."

Two of the Scouts went to him along with two of his delegation and each took a limb and stretched him out on the ground.

"Specialist Bigsly, wake him and once he is fully awake, castrate him, remove his tail, then shave his mane off him. Do not let him bleed out as I am not done with him."

"Yes Lord Carlos." Jeniree replied. She went into the shuttle and returned moments later with the Shuttle's first-aid/surgical kit.

Tamas translated Carlos's words to the Council causing an outcry from the Council members.

"Silence!" Carlos ordered.

Jeniree first cut Moshe's short pants exposing his manhood to the word, then waved an inhaler under his nose to wake him up. When fully awake he tried to fight the people holing him down but without success. Carlos walked over so Moshe could see him.

"This is for Marta. Do it Specialist."

Jeniree reached in and grabbed Moshe's scrotum causing him to howl, then with a pair of vibra-scissors, cut his scrotum from his groin, then held it up for all to see. Many of the bystanders howled at the sight of Moshe's scrotum knowing he could no longer breed with a female.

"Don't loose those things Jeniree, I have a plan for them."

She acknowledged her instructions then sprayed a wound sealant on the bleeding remains of his manhood before telling those holding Moshe down to roll him over. She cut his tail off the same way and treated the open wound to prevent infection.

Once that was out of the way, she straddled his back and using the scissors, she cut his mane as close as she could as everyone could hear him crying, begging her to stop.

When Jeniree finished, she stood, still straddling Moshe and asked what she was to do with his manhood. Carlos told her to bag everything up and just hang on to it, then ordered Moshe to be released. Carlos kicked him in the side to get his attention.

"Look upon your tormentor Moshe. The one who removed your manhood was a female, just as the one you humiliated that pledged herself to you and bonded with you. Your manhood will be taken to Marta's family and it will be proclaimed that she has her honor back and your child will never know the name of the creature that planted his seed into her mother. Yes, Moshe, Marta is bearing another daughter because that is the seed you gave her to grow inside of her."

Moshe just lay in the street holding his abused groin as Carlos walked over to Tamas.

"Tamas, you will guide Jeniree and Vanna to Marta's family and you will tell them what I told Moshe. He stole her honor and I am giving it back to her family. She kept her pledge

97

with Moshe and he abused it and her. Tell them that I, Lord Carlos Gannaway, will insure Marta is cared for and treated with the respect she is due, and Tamas, you lie to her family, you try to make Moshe a victim here and you will be the next victim of Jeniree's cuts. Do you understand me Tamas?"

"Yes, Lord Carlos, it will be done as you require."

"Before you leave, tell the Council we will meet again tomorrow to discuss treating with your people and mine. What I did today was to keep a promise, an oath I made when I first met Moshe and he assaulted Marta as she was protecting my life with her body. No male has the right to treat a female, bonded or not in the manner Moshe treated Marta. Not in my universe, or yours. Tell them to go in peace and meet with me in peace tomorrow as I have had my fill of anger and hatred. Do it now Tamas then leave to do as I instructed."

Tamas deeply bowed before turning to the Council. When he finished speaking, the Council members bowed to Carlos and quietly left. Tamas indicated for Jeniree to follow as Vanna fell in behind her. As Vanna passed Carlos, she told him the other two females were following along still cloaked. Carlos just nodded and turned back to the shuttle.

Doctor Bradford had collected up the first-aid box and was waiting for Carlos at the ramp and treated his wounds.

"Carlos, give this a couple of days and I'll fix it so there is no scaring."

"No Zachery, let them scar as a reminder of my mistake in not killing Moshe when I first met him. To remind me of the mistakes of my youth as I grow old."

Bradford just nodded as he treated the wounds. Carlos looked over to where Marta was standing and it seemed she had a smile on her face, even though she still had her head down in submission.

Once Bradford had completed his treatment of Carlos, Carlos went over to the Scout ship and instructed them to take Moshe to the furthest of their farm planets and leave him there with only his skin to protect himself with. He could live or die by his own hands. The Scout put restraints on Moshe so he could not harm them, then carried him aboard their ship and lifted off. It would not matter if they had restrained him or not as Moshe was broken, only a weak shadow of his former self.

The human delegation loaded up into the shuttle with Marta so she could be taken to the Creedmoor's hospital for examination. Carlos went directly to his quarters and laid down, knowing that before the day was over, he would have to contact his Aunt and explain to the Throne his actions.

It was nearly an hour before he heard his crystal signaling for his attention. He activated his crystal and watched as two sets of holograms appeared before him. One was his parents, the other was his aunt.

"You Highness, Mother, Father."

"Carlos Gannaway, before I let your parents take their share of your flesh, I want to know what the hell you were thinking engaging that animal as you did?"

"Your Highness…"

"Don't Your Highness me Nephew."

"Aunt Consuela, Connie, I knew I could take Moshe, and I knew I was going to get hurt in doing it, but I knew I could take him. I did so to avenge Marta and keep my oath concerning what I would do if he harmed her. I did it because I deserved the pain I suffered for not killing him the first time I met him."

"I've spoken to Demetri and he feels the Council is now in a position to talk now instead of stalling. Was this in your thoughts or did Demetri just try to fill in the gaps when I talked to him a few minutes ago?"

"No, that was on my mind also as I told him before meeting Moshe in the street."

"Lucen, your turn." Connie advised her brother, Carlos's father.

"Carlos, I don't think I have to say anything as your aunt has fairly well covered it, but son, as stupid a stunt that was, I am proud of you for defending the young lady, and returning her honor to her family. Now what are your plans?"

Carlos went over the plans he was considering as he lay on the bed, waiting for the contact with them. His plans were accepted with slight modifications and the contact was broken with the knowledge that when the sun came up the next morning, more ships would be in orbit above the planet.

Vanna reported in later advising that Marta's family had Moshe's manhood and accepted that their honor had been restored. She told Carlos that they had talked with Tamas about the root that Moshe had used to cause Marta's near catatonic state and he provided them with a large sample which they had already given to Doctor Bradford to analyze.

He was taking his evening meal in his quarters when Doctor Bradford came to report on his examination of Marta.

"First of all the baby is in good health even with her being fed that damn root. Right now we do not know if the effects are temporary or cumulative, only time will tell us that."

"And the rest of her injuries?"

"I want to send her back to Altair and let our genetic specialists work on her. Since there is no bone to interfere, it might be possible to regrow her tongue, but that is for them to determine. Now in domestic felines, the removal of their claws in

100

such a manner is permanent, but her fingers can be repair from the damage of the claws being ripped out of her fingers."

He paused for a moment.

"Carlos, what do you want to do?"

"I've already talked to the Throne this afternoon. My plans will become public tomorrow, but keep her comfortable and give her what she needs. I placed her in the position she found herself in and my honor demands I attend to her needs anyway I can."

Later that evening, Jeniree came to Carlos's quarters to check on his injuries. He sat patiently as she once again cleaned his chest and doctored his claw marks the checked on the ones on his arm. When she finished, she reached up, pulled his face to hers and kissed him for a long time before leaning back from him.

"Carlos, I know you would prefer Sabrina in your bed, but I think you will find me a good substitute for a night."

Carlos looked at her for a moment then pulled her back to him and kissed her.

Meeting in the Middle

The meeting the next day went much better that previous meetings as the Council was willing to listen to what might be to their world's benefit. The only sour point in the meeting was when one of the Councilmen asked what had happened to Moshe after they had left.

When Carlos explained what he had ordered done with Moshe, a protest arouse of how could he take care of himself without his wives. Carlos drove home the point he had been trying to make from day one.

"How will Moshe survive without his wives? Do you hear yourselves speak such words? The females we bond and mate with give us warmth in our beds on a cold night. They suffer the birth of our children, our offspring so we might have our name carried forward. They cook our food and maintain our home for us. And you sit there and do not allow females to enter this building. You place yourselves over the very individuals that gave you life. In my universe, the females are equal to the males, and we males understand if they give themselves to us, it is because they desire it so."

Tamas translated twice as he carefully thought through what Carlos has said. There was no way for Carlos to check Tamas's translation but from the fear in his eyes the previous day, Carlos felt Tamas was afraid of making a mistake in translation.

One of the aliens asked a question which Tamas had to translate. He thought for several seconds before speaking to Carlos.

"Lord Carlos, you have defeated one of our best warriors with ease. You have warriors that can vanish before our eyes. You have great ships above us in space. We cannot stand against your might. What do you require of us?"

"Tamas, express for me that the fight between myself and Moshe was personal and had nothing to do with why I came to your world. If he had not abused Marta, he would still be in his home with his wives including Marta."

Tamas translated with the Council member nodding his acceptance of his statement.

"Now, please express that just because we have ships of war in space above your world, we are not here as invaders. Our warriors only came to the surface yesterday to insure the fight between myself and Moshe was not interfered with by your people. They have lifted from your world with only our shuttle crew on the surface."

Tamas once more translated, stopped in translation and started again as he felt he had it wrong.

"So to answer what I require from this world is simple in many ways, but will take much effort on your part."

He had Tamas translate that part before continuing.

"In my universe, when I defeated Moshe all he had now belongs to me including his wives and offspring. First of all, Marta will be taken to Doctor Bradford's world where she will repaired, fixed as best the Doctor's there can do. It is my responsibility for this to happen since I taught her about my universe which Moshe felt was threatening and cause him to treat her as he did."

Carlos waited as Tamas spoke to the Council.

"Now, once today's meeting is over, Tamas I will need you to go with my female warriors to Moshe's home and gather up his wives and off spring. They will be sent to the world we call Zyra, which is Lord Demetri's home world to be educated and trained in the ways of my universe. When they are fully educated, they will return to educate your world in our ways so you will better understand what life in the universe is really like."

Tamas translated, stopped asked Carlos a question, then finished translating. Carlos was waiting for the Council to blow up from what he was suggesting but they just sat waiting for the other boot to drop.

Another Councilman asked a question directly of Carlos.

"Lord Carlos, what of yourself? Are you going to construct a palace here to rule over us from?"

Demetri let out a light chuckle and Carlos had to strain to keep from laughing.

"No, I will leave here to allow you to rule as before considering what I said about your females being equal to you. I know it will be hard for you at first, but I believe you are able to do this thing."

He gave Tamas a chance to translate, then Tamas asked a question for himself.

"Lord Carlos, what if we need your help in these things?"

"Lord Mewa gave me the rights to surface mine the world I found Marta on. With the approval of the Council, I will build a home there and mine the world giving consideration to the animals on that world."

Tamas spoke to the Council who then talked amongst themselves for several minutes before Mewa spoke up.

"Lord Carlos, that world is yours to do with as you please. We only ask that we can harvest meat from that world as we need to feed our people."

"Lord Mewa, I shall protect the animals on what I will call Marta's World and will welcome your hunters to harvest that which your world needs but do not withhold that food, the meat from your females. You will find they will grown stronger to help you if they can eat as you do."

Once more the Council talked amongst themselves before Mewa once again spoke up.

"Lord Carlos, we shall honor your words and feed our females as we also feed. Is this all?"

"No, but it is enough for this day. We have recorded our discussion today and will provide a copy of it with a machine to view the talks in case we need to be certain of what has been agreed upon."

The meeting broke up with the Council staying in the room to further talk amongst themselves. Tamas was met outside by Vanna and her team and they took another shuttle to Moshe's home. Tamas took some time persuading the wives they had to go with the Centaurian women and that Moshe would never come home again.

Vanna made Tamas to go up to the Destroyer Conway with them and the family so he could give them basic instructions before the Conway boosted out of orbit for Zyra. When the wives asked where Marta was, Vanna explained through Tamas that she was on another ship which had already left for a different world than they were going to for medical treatment.

Eight Centaurians that were on the Conway were introduced to the wives and Tamas explained for Vanna they would assist them during their trip and also help them learn more about speaking Fed Speak and how to use the computers to learn from. Tamas had to explain to the wives they had to stay within the areas the ship's personal said they could go and that included the children.

Tamas returned to the surface with Vanna and her team and thanked them for letting him see the ship. He then went to the Council and told them what he had seen of the human's ship in comparison to their own ships. This further reinforced the strength the humans had brought to their worlds.

Demetri waited until they were in Carlos's quarters before he spoke of the deal Carlos had wrangled from the Council concerning what would be known as Marta's World.

"Carlos, unless your aunt says otherwise, you just conned those people out of a planet and it's riches. And in doing so, you just bypassed the Federation's Articles for Prospecting meaning you own one hundred percent of the wealth of the planet."

"Demetri, the Throne will not complain and my aunt will step on any bureaucrat that tries to say otherwise. The video record will show I only asked to mine the planet, and they gave the whole planet to me. Regardless of how I obtained it, forty percent of the wealth of the planet after today will go into the Marta Foundation which was established last night. It will duplicate the efforts of the Hanover Foundation, but for the purpose of helping these people grow and thrive."

Demetri laughed hard at what he realized what Carlos had done. If the Council had not given him title to the world, they would be lucky to see five percent of the riches from it, but now they would have the best part of thirty percent after management expenses.

"What have you made from that world already?"

Carlos went to his safe and opened it, removing a file from it and handing it to Demetri. Demetri's eyes got big and he laughed again.

"Carlos, your father told me you set out to make something of yourself, away from the family business. You've accomplished that and more."

"Yes, but I have paid a high price for it. Higher than I ever figured on paying."

Other Considerations

The were still questions that both Carlos and the Throne wanted answered. One was concerning the human that had taught Tamas Fed Speak. The other was concerning the off spring of the rap of the aliens by human raiders or slavers. Carlos addressed the human language teacher directly to Tamas.

Tamas took Carlos and Demetri to what could best be described as a zoo. In one portion of it was a small abode and sitting outside of it was a grey haired human in a brown robe. The human's hair was long, needing cut along with a beard which nearly went down to his waist. The human looked out through the bars of his cage a long time at Carlos before standing up and walking to the bars.

"Are you for real?" The human asked.

"Yes, my name is Carlos Gannaway, and I am very real?"

"Gannaway, Gannaway; as in Prince Gannaway?"

"I'm his grandson. Who are you?"

"Ralph Childress. You're armed. Are you here to rescue me?"

Demetri punched Ralph's name into his pad. Moments later his name popped up and Demetri handed the pad over to Carlos. Carlos read the data then turned to Tamas.

"Tamas, according to this, Ralph was a licensed prospector, not a raider or slaver. Release him immediately or I will."

Tamas barked orders at one of the keepers in this zoo and they took off in search of who had the keys to Ralph's cage. It was a few minutes later that Ralph's cage was unlocked and he stepped out of it to freedom. He fell to his knees in front of Carlos and began to cry.

"Thank you Sire, you have no idea how it has been in that place."

Carlos reached down and picked him up.

"Stand Mister Childress. Stand as a free man once more."

Carlos motioned to one of the Marines standing back, watching over Carlos and Demetri.

"Mister Childress, go with this Marine. He will take you to our shuttle and from there, we will later go up to our ship so you can get a physical, get cleaned up and something to eat."

Childress was led off by the Marine as Carlos walked into the cage, then into the small hut Childress had been living in. He walked back out and looked at Tamas.

"No human, not even a slaver should live in such conditions. I will expect the Council to make reparations to Ralph for his time in that cage. Tell the council that and find out what happened to his ship. It will be returned to him. Do I have to repeat myself Tamas?"

"No Lord Carlos, I will see to it today."

"Good Tamas, now what of the off spring of those females that were raped. Violated?"

"I will get you the information on how to find the world they were taken too also today."

"Very good Tamas. We shall take Ralph to our ship and later return to receive the information we need."

"Yes Lord Carlos."

When they returned to the surface, Tamas showed them where Ralph's ship was located and Carlos ordered the Creedmoor's Engineering Chief down to inspect the ship for flight worthiness. Carlos instructed the Chief to do what was necessary with the ship and to present him with the bill for parts and labor which he would in turn present to the Council as part of the reparations to Mister Childress for his imprisonment.

As they prepared to break orbit for the world where the others were being held, Demetri and Bradford were in Carlos's room sipping of brandy, discussing what had occurred with Bradford brought up something he felt was interesting. Especially since Marta was enroute to Altair and the wives to Zyra.

"Carlos, the genetic folks on Altair are required to read a book written before man first took to the sky. It's about a mad scientist who transforms animals into a new species of a mix of human and animal characteristics. It warns of the tampering with humanity and the possible results. Could we be seeing something similar here on these worlds?"

"I know the book Zachery, and it makes you wonder if the author knew more than he was supposed to know. The Throne is sending a scientific team to the ruins up in the North to find out what they can about these people. I have been authorized to send Scout ships to all of the worlds claimed by these people to sensor survey each planet for precious metals and other metals and minerals which can provide them some margin of wealth to improve their existence."

"Carlos, you know it would be a lot easier talking about those people if they had a name for their planet. They don't even have a name for each specific species. That needs to be addressed in time."

"Yeah, Marta just called them the People. So I forgot to ask, what arrangements did you make for Marta during her trip to Altair?"

"I arranged for four female Centaurian medics to accompany her so she would feel as comfortable as possible since they are similar to her in form. She seemed to understand what was happening to her, but the effects of the root or drug in her was still keeping her emotions down. But when I told her that the baby was in good condition, it seemed she smiled, then went back to her blank look."

"Zachery, she is or was very intelligent. I suspect once the females of these people are allowed some freedom and are allowed to learn, be educated, the men will find themselves in trouble."

"Well Carlos, isn't that universal?"

Everyone laughed and changed the subject. Later that evening Jeniree returned to Carlos's quarters.

The Outcasts

Orbiting what was called Habitat Number Three, the Creedmoor's sensors picked up one major location where the people of this world was located with a few structures spread out near it. There were fields of food plants growing near those outlying building which Carlos and crew figured were farms. The people on this world might be considered outcasts by the others, but they seemed more organized in their efforts to fend for themselves.

When they dropped to the surface, they were greeted by both male and female inhabitants carrying crudely crafted spears and swords. Demetri was the first out of the shuttle which seemed to ease the tension present in the inhabitants considering he looked like the majority of the awaiting group of people.

Carlos and Doctor Bradford were the next off the shuttle and they just stood at the bottom of the ramp, waiting for the inhabitants to make the first move. An elderly human female moved through the crowd and came forward to meet them. She slightly bowed before speaking in Fed Speak.

"Your shuttle shows Fleet markings. Are you Federation officers?"

Demetri indicated Carlos.

"This is Lord Carlos Gannaway, and we do represent the Federation and the Fleet. Who might you be, Madam?"

"I am Freda. I was captured when the raiders I was associated with came to these worlds. What are you doing on this world?"

Carlos stepped forward.

"Freda, we have came to check on what the others consider outcasts. We have come to advise you that the Federation is slowly moving into this part of the universe and to see what you need to survive until further arrangements can be made to take care of you."

Freda thought for a moment.

"I see you have an Altairian with you. We do have some medical needs, but other than help growing our food crops, we have survived as you see us. But let's go someplace were we can talk in comfort instead of under the sun."

Freda took them to a large, open shelter where they sat and shared a fruity tea as Freda gave them a list of things that would help their community. The people here were a mixture of Centaurian like individuals and humans.

She finally spoke of her own situation in that she had been a prostitute on Spencer when she joined the raiders. She figured servicing a dozen men on a ship was better than what she was doing and it would give her a chance to leave Spencer and maybe find a better life elsewhere.

Freda said the raiders treated her better and she learned some engineering from them until they ventured into this part of space and were captured. She estimated she had been on this world for over twenty years and had taught Fed Speak to its citizens along with what farming she remembered from being raised on a farm.

They took a tour of the nearest farm and Carlos noted they had done well using an ox like creature native to this world as an animal to pull their crude, wooden plows to turn the soil. Carlos took a hard look at the small forge they had built and the metals they were using to forge knives, and spear heads for hunting game.

When Carlos mentioned taking the humans from this world, Freda stopped him there and told him this was her home and she had a purpose in life. She had two children here, one conceived by her rape by one of the Kats that had came to deposit

112

others, and one by a male half-bred she had mated with. She was not leaving, but would be thankful for what help the Federation could provide.

Freda and Carlos made up a list of needs, and he notified the Creedmoor to send down what they had available and the rest would come in time once those items could be package and shipped to them. When Freda commented they had no way to pay for the equipment to further improve their farming, Carlos just smiled and told her the Marta Foundation would pay for those things, but later on, once they were more modernized, they could possibly mine for minerals the sensors showed was present on the planet to pay for greater improvements.

They stayed on this world for three days as medical teams gave each individual a physical and treated injuries or illnesses as needed. One key thing the physicals did was give Carlos a solid headcount of the inhabitants of the planet. Before they lifted back to the Creedmoor, Carlos asked the name of the planet and found they had not named it. He suggested they name the world so when referencing it in communications it would be clear who everyone was talking about.

Through Demetri, Freda had learned how the Federation had entered this part of space by Carlos prospecting the worlds. She called a meeting of the eldest members of the community to determine a name for their world. They named it Gannaway after Carlos.

Once back on the Creedmoor, Carlos packaged everything he had learned about this world now named after his family along with the list of things needed by the inhabitants and sent it to the Throne via his crystal.

Demetri looked at the crystal, even picking it up once Carlos was finished and examined it.

"Carlos, I've seen these used for decades now and have yet to figure out how they work."

"You're not alone Demetri. I asked my father once about them and he said that only the technicians who make them know how they work and it is the closest kept secret in the universe. The technicians will not even talk about how they were chosen to work on the crystals. The crystal itself is somewhat rare with its chemical makeup, but that alone does not make it a communications crystal. Its what the technicians do to it once in their labs that is the secret."

"Each crystal is produced for a specific individual or group of individuals by DNA, which is confusing enough as it is. The ones on ships are keyed to the coding of that specific ships communications system, which even the Creedmoor's comm specialist will tell you they have no idea how that works. But knowing the crystal's chemical makeup, a prospector can get rich if he stumbles on a good source for them."

"Yeah Carlos, and you found a very rich vein of those crystals."

Carlos just smiled and let the subject drop where it was at.

Marta's World

Carlos felt he had done all he could do and returned to Marta's World to consider building a home for himself there since he now owned the planet as per Council decree. He had insured communications devices were in place at both the alien's world and on Gannaway with instructors to teach them how to use the devices.

Buoy's were set out from the edge of the alien worlds warning anyone that these systems were under Federation Protection and the Throne had a Fleet patrolling this region of space to prevent any trespassers.

Carlos was living in his ship trying to determine where to build and exactly what to build when he was visited by a Fleet officer.

"Lord Carlos, I am Lieutenant Commander Zumwalt, and I have brought my engineers here to build you a home and landing facilities as per orders from the Throne."

"Commander Zumwalt, I have no idea where or what I want built, but you can start here with the landing facilities were you can bring down your heavy equipment if needed. But understand you are not building a Port of Call for the Fleet."

"Yes Lord Carlos, I have been so advise not to build that which would interfere with the natural movement of creatures here on the planet, just a place so freighters and such can land from time to time."

"Thank you Commander, and once I figure out where and what I am going to build, I will let you know. Also, there is no prohibition on hunting for fresh meat for your crews but advise me beforehand. I promised the original owners of this world I would see to the herds which provides them their meats."

"I understand Lord Carlos, I had best get busy surveying the site then get my people to work."

The Engineers built two heavy-duty landing pads large enough for Fleet Replenishment freighters or the heavy Construction freighters along with road beds to an staging area. They cleaned up after themselves leaving no debris to interfere with the appearance of the planet.

The Marines that supported the Engineers as security took two large cows with Carlos's approval and they had them cooked over an open pit once the work was done. By this time Carlos had his mind made up where to build his home.

First he had Marta's habitat closed with a steel access door so no animals could find it and move in or damage it. He then moved down from the habitat five hundred meters and laid out where he wanted his home. At first he just wanted a simple house to live in but after a conversation with his mother, he decided to make sure there were rooms for guests or even children when the time came.

Ten hectares was fenced in by a stone masonry wall just over a meter high to prevent animals from traversing the site. The house itself was a single story structure built from native granite. Carlos watched the construction realizing this was also a home that could be defended against anyone determined to cause him harm. There were even intrusion sensors all along the wall perimeter to alert him of trespassers.

Electricity was provided by both solar panels on the roof plus a fusion generator place in a small bunker at the rear of the property. Water came from a well drilled into limestone which made it nearly pure from the well head, but still ran through a filter before entering the house.

It was as he was slowly setting up the interior of the house, that an event occurred that upset him the most. A half-company, two sections of Lancers landed with written orders from the Throne to provide him with security on or off the planet. He was polite with the Senior Lieutenant in charge then placed a call to the Throne.

"Your Highness, would you care to advise me why my home looks like a fortified bunker and I now had two sections of Lancers on my front lawn?"

"Well Carlos you are much more polite than I estimated you would be in making this contact. So let me put it too you in this manner."

She paused for a moment before continuing.

"Lord Carlos Gannaway, your current situation in a very real sense makes you the Federation Ambassador to these new, unnamed words. It is the responsibility of the Throne and the Federation to insure your safety at all times as our Ambassador, especially considering the primitive nature of the people you have to deal with as Ambassador. There is also the one called Moshe that needs to be addressed. You may have removed him as a threat to your safety, but we must consider his family and those friends who might seek revenge against you. Now do you question the Thrones responsibility in these things?"

"No Your Highness, I do not."

"Carlos, as your aunt, the family would still take steps to insure your safety. This goes far beyond your prospecting a new world."

"Thank you Aunt Consuela, I now understand my place in this. It seems we of Denoyelles blood are cursed and karma places one of us where we have to lead the fight for those who cannot. I used the idea of prospecting to run from destiny only to have it laid in my lap. I only hope that history will show I tried to uphold the family's name."

Consuela was quiet for a moment as if thinking.

"There are exceptions to every rule, even within the Principles of Leadership, although those exceptions are extremely rare and must be with honor. From this day forward, Earl Carlos Gannaway, you shall be known as Baron Carlos Gannaway, Ambassador to the New Worlds."

"Thank you, your Highness, even if I do not feel I have earned such an honor. I stand ready to represent the Throne to these new worlds."

The contact was broken from the Throne leaving Carlos with more questions than answers, but he had been raised near the Throne and understood that was often how business was done. He went to the Lancers and showed them a location to the rear of his estate for them to have a barracks and facilities built, then just left them to their duties as he knew better than to interfere with them.

But with the arrival of the Lancers returned his thinking to having someone to share his home with him. Vanna and Jeniree had both kept him company for a time but they had recently shipped out without ever joining with him on the surface. Sabrina kept returning to his mind yet he could not find the courage to send her a message to return to him. Carlos was actually afraid she would say no after her failed marriage.

It seemed that time had paused for a short time as Carlos discovered he enjoyed gardening, planting flowers plus a small vegetable garden around and behind his house. But as he was turning the soil on the west side of his house for a flower bed, he turned up a large nugget of gold which reminded him why he had came here in the first place. He had to make the world a productive investment even if he had already made his riches, but how was another question.

He called for Commander Zumwalt of the Engineers in for a long discussion starting just after the midday meal and lasted well into the night. They determined two problems. First was getting talented people out this far from known space to work the mines. Second was getting people he could trust not to pocket more than was reasonable of the raw minerals, especially the crystals.

Zumwalt suggested retired Fleet Engineers who knew how to rip into the earth and how to return it back to a reasonable norm and had already been processed through Fleet Intelligence for clearances. Carlos gave Zumwalt the go ahead to publish a notice in the Fleet news network that he was looking for twenty able bodied men and women to come work for him. They had checked the Federation Labor boards on the average wages for a miner, and Carlos upped it twenty percent plus room and board.

Carlos was able to arrange for all prospective miners to report to his father who had each individual ran through a physical before contracting a ship to take them to Marta's World. Eight had families which meant Carlos had to arrange for teacher's to also come and deal with the education of the children.

Life on this new world suddenly became more complicated and crowded. But life elsewhere was growing.

Marta had her baby during the transit to Altair. It was as predicted and female child and it was covered in black fur much like her father. Carlos looked at the hologram of Marta holding the infant and noticed the scars on her face had been removed by the ships surgeon.

One of the medics attending to Marta wrote that she was coming out of her stupor and had used a pad to spell out the name of the child. She was named Tikka.

Being the Ambassador to the New Worlds as they were being referenced in dispatches, Carlos found himself in possession of a new, high speed Destroyer Escort as his method of transport away from Marta's World. It carried four of the Navy's version of the Hornet fighter/bomber that his father had helped design and implement into the Fleet.

Once he had his miners on the ground, his next problem was what to focus on first. This was resolved by the family's agent on Hayuta who sent him a list of minerals by priority demand. Carlos handed the list off to the senior retired Master Chief and showed him the location of the crystals the Hayutan labs wanted due to their purity.

Carlos also learned that of the near metric ton of crystals he had already picked up and shipped, only thirty-two percent were viable for use as communications crystals. But that percentage was well worth the expense as the sale of said crystals was by the metric ton. And those not used in communications found their way into other items, both technical and cosmetic such as prisms.

It had been over a solar year since Carlos had entertained a female in his bed and he was gathering the strength to ask Sabrina to join him. As the ancient script went, the best laid plans.

Disappointment

Carlos returned from the Home World after meeting with the Council to help them draft a charter for their people to find a shuttle on the pad in front of his home. As he exited his own shuttle, he found Vanna waiting for him and she was not smiling as she greeted him.

"You don't look pleased to see me Vanna. What's up?"

"Carlos there is no way to say this so I will be blunt. Sabrina is dead. She was leading a mission outside the Western Rim against a slaver colony when she caught a slug in the head that penetrated her helmet. Carlos, she died instantly according to what the report says from her medic."

Carlos went numb at the thought of Sabrina dying. His own lack of courage in such matters led to this point. He thought that if he had asked her when he first returned to Marta's World to come to him, she would still be alive.

"Vanna, I was going to ask her to marry me, but I could never gather the courage to do that after she had gone through a bad marriage."

"Carlos, I talked to Sabrina before she left about you. She was in love with you but felt that it would be a bad move for both of you if she stayed here. She had actually requested transfer away from here, from you so you could find someone better suited to you. I never really understood what she meant by that, but she had her reasons."

"Thank you Vanna for coming to tell me about Sabrina. I often felt there was something under the surface with our relationship, but never asked."

"Carlos, what is it with you men of Denoyelles blood? It seems you are as brave as any human in face of danger, but when it comes to women, almost weak as a kitten."

"We're raised with the prospect of a woman who only want's the titles and money that goes with the name. My sister was no different as men hunted her for the wealth she has available. According to my father, Aunt Consuela was years in finding a man who wanted her for just herself. Uncle Frederick is a good man, and takes good care of her. This is part of the family curse Vanna, and it makes us leery of those we take to our bed."

"Yet you have taken myself and my entire team to bed at one time or another."

"Vanna, Count Conrad wrote in his personal journal that he picked Centaurian females as his security and fake concubine because of the honor Centaurians embrace. You only went to bed with me because that was what you desired, not the hopes of getting your hands on any possible wealth I may have due to my family. There has been many Centaurians marry into the family but it was for love, not wealth."

"I know Carlos, and if it wasn't for the reason I am here today, I would consider going to your bed once again, but that would not do you any good as we both know. Now for the truth. News of Sabrina's death has been classified by the Throne because the Princess knew of your relationship with her. I was sent here by the Throne to break the news to you because the Princess knew we were also close. I hate being the one to bring you that news but I could not tell the Princess no."

"It's alright Vanna, my father told me that I lived under a microscope and that my life was under observation. It is one of the reasons I came out here by myself, but I have the feeling, have always had the feeling of being watched, even out here."

"I'm really sorry Carlos. About Sabrina, and about how you feel you have to live your life. Once more to be honest, if you were not part of the ruling family of the Federation, I could find it easy to fall in love with you and make you a happy man. But I don't want that kind of life. Maybe that was what Sabrina was talking about, I don't know. Nothing in your life is simple and that is too much for me to consider, but Carlos, you are a good man, try to find your center and enjoy this life, it's all we have before us."

Vanna gave Carlos a deep kiss then walked away, back to her shuttle and the life she preferred to live. Carlos went into his house once she was gone and sat for a long time thinking about what Vanna had said to him. He drank a tall glass of Hayutan Scotch, then went to bed knowing he had to find a way to live without the specter of his family over him. Yet he had already surpassed his own father's wealth which made him an even larger target for females with rich tastes.

He had to laugh at the thought of being chased by gold digging females since the only females on this world actually dug gold and other riches from the soil under his employment. Or were members of the Fleet. Who or where was he going to find a good woman to settle down with?

Just before sleep took him, he remembered his grandmother had once been a Fleet Master Chief Electrician.

The Passage of Time

Regardless of happiness or heart break, life moves on with the passage of time. Carlos was getting updates concerning Marta and her education plus the growth and reattachment of her tongue and tail by the genetics lab on Altair. She was going through speech therapy learning once again to speak and she refused to vid-chat with Carlos until she felt she was going to be as good in her speech as possible.

When she learned of Sabrina's death, she sent him a message telling him how sorry she felt for his loss and for him to move on with his life and find another to love. Carlos knew Marta was being watched over by Centaurians and the way she structured her message told him of their influence in her life.

The Hanover Foundation brought in teachers and engineers to help the aliens of the New Worlds improve their situation. The inhabitants of Gannaway were the most eager to learn and utilize the farming equipment brought to the planet. They even suggested that the Fleet build a base on the planet on the second continent.

The Fleet built a staging area on the second continent which also acted as protection for the inhabitants from any possible raiders which might pass through the region of space.

The aliens never could decide on a name for their world and just accepted the use of New World's and went from there. Carlos thought it was interesting that they never differentiated between the different species of individuals on their world as they considered themselves all related.

It was over a year after Carlos opened the New Worlds to the Federation that a scientific team arrived to dig out the ruins in the frozen north. It was estimated it would take as many as five years to clear the ice and snow enough to begin proper examination of the ruins. The reason for such a lengthy process was to prevent damage to the ruins and artifacts from being too eager to open them for research.

Within three years, Carlos had to increase his employee base to provide for the demands being put upon him for the minerals and crystals from Marta's World. Part of the slow down in providing those things was his determination to return the surface of the world to its natural state as much as possible.

Any areas that had to be deforested for mining was replanted as soon as possible. This required him to establish a nursery to grow tree sprigs for planting which required more space and employees. He built the nurseries on the third continent which had sparse animal life on it. It was also on this continent that he drilled for petroleum for the use in producing plastics. A heavy landing field was built to accommodate the fuel tankers/freighters which landed to haul the raw petroleum to the refineries and factories demanding the product.

Carlos sat looking at his accounts realizing he was wealthier than his wildest dreams. He had a dozen businesses from his inheritance that was making him wealthy but the mining operations on Marta's World was far beyond his immediate family's wealth. He began dumping off millions of Crowns into the Hanover Foundation and the Marta Foundation just to get it off his books even if he exceeded the allowable tax deduction.

His bonuses to his employees made several wealthy in their own right and he found that they were also giving to the Foundations as they followed his example.

But as he entered his fifth year in business, he found himself facing a new foe. A foe he could not face as he had Moshe, but one that came with a sharp pencil and an attitude.

Excuse me!!

Carlos was warned in advance of the pending audit of his mining operation. His books were maintained on Hollis by the same firm that kept his father's books, but this audit was because there were questions concerning the business expenditures Carlos was claiming on his taxes.

His father warned him not to attempt to hide anything from the auditor because there was nothing he nor Carlos's aunt could do to cover him since the auditor was from the Federation Auditor's Office and those people were noted for their honesty and thoroughness.

He had a complete copy of his accounts which were to be a duplicate of the one's that the auditor was to pick up on Hollis while enroute to Marta's World. The only difference in them was he downloaded his records the morning of the arrival of the auditor which were now three months newer than the ones they had.

Carlos was standing by the gate to his estate with four Lancers when the shuttle bearing the auditor landed on the guest pad. Only one person left the shuttle and this took Carlos by surprise. It was a tall, blond haired Altairian, wearing a bulky jump suit so as not to give away her assets and she walked as if she heading to the gallows.

One of the Lancers gave a light whistle as they admired the female walking towards them. There was no doubt this was one very attractive woman but the sour look on her face did not distract from her beauty.

"Yeah, I agree." Carlos whispered to the Lancer before he moved forward to greet the auditor.

He stopped and met her a few feet away from his previous position and offered his hand.

"I am Carlos Gannaway, welcome to Marta's World. And you are?"

She looked at Carlos's offered hand then back at him without taking it.

"I am Deyanna Marcos. I'm here to audit you."

"Yeah, I figured that much Miss Marcos. It is Miss is it not?"

"Yes, it is Miss. Now where can I set up and get this over with?"

"Follow me please."

Carlos led her into the estate and into the house. He had moved the bed and things out of one bedroom and turned it into a temporary office for her to use. She asked for his current set of books and he passed over the micro-disc containing that mornings download. She took it as if it was dirty then told him if she needed to ask him any questions, she would call for him.

Two hours later she called him in to ask him about the cost of building his home. Carlos pointed out that it was ordered by the Throne and there was a notation where he had reimbursed the Fleet for the time and materials expended in building the estate. Any specific charges would have to be obtained from the Throne as all he received was the total which he authorized immediate payment.

When she asked about the Lancers and their facilities, he pointed out that expense was not being billed for as it was being paid for by Princess Consuela from family funds and she would have to check with the Princess concerning those expenses.

But she really dug her spurs into Carlos when she noticed the expenditure for certain pieces of heavy equipment listed at a higher price than she felt was necessary. Carlos said he left the purchase of heavy equipment to his mining chiefs since they had experience with the equipment. Marcos asked why he was spending more money from one of his family's competitors then buying from his family at a discount?

Carlos called in his mining chief who explained that the controls on the equipment they purchased was simpler to operate and maintain in the environment they were working in. Without a heavy maintenance facility, the Bellus manufactured equipment would sit longer waiting for parts than the equipment from Woodford. The overall savings came from usage hours, not from the purchase price. Marcos had no choice but accept that argument and moved on to other things.

Even though Carlos offered Marcos a room, she lifted back to her transport nightly, taking everything with her to insure he could not tamper with her work.

She refused all offers of refreshment during her time on planet and he noticed she drank water from the adjacent bathroom in a special cup with could detect impurities or drugs. For her midday meal, she ate a Fleet ration bar she had brought with her. Carlos finally gave up trying to be nice to her and just let things happen.

After a week of going over his books, she wanted to see the actually mining operations. Her questions concerning such operations was the expenses he was showing covering the return of the mining areas back to as close to original as possible. When she questioned his restoration of the land as she stood on a site where gold had been mined, he told her that he had promised the Council of the New World's he would take care of the land. He pointed to a herd of animals passing close by and told her that it was important to the food supply of the New World's that he kept his promise.

At every turn she tried to find a reason to impose penalties against his taxes and income but he was able to counter each attempt. She even showed him where he was donating more that allowable to the Marta Foundation, yet he was only taking the deduction allowed. When she asked him he had a simple reply.

"How much money does a person need? I have more than I can ever spend now. Besides, the Foundation will put the money to good use helping the people of the New World's advance and progress."

She ended her audit after a week in her make-shift office then returned to her transport to write her report. Three days later she returned to hand him a copy of the report stating she found zero discrepancies in his books except for the larger than allowable donation to the Marta Foundation which he had not tried to claim on his taxes.

He accepted the report and as he started to go to his office with it she spoke again, but not about his audit.

"Baron Gannaway, why is it you have not made a pass at me?"

"Excuse me?"

"Every man I have audited have made passes at me. Unsuccessful passes, but they have tried. Do you find something wrong with me?"

"Miss Marcos, you were sent here to audit my books, my accounts, not to play destroy my bed sheets. There is no doubt you are an attractive woman, but your entire attitude has been one of stay away from me. Another time or place, I most likely would have tried to get to know you better, not in the let's jump into my bed better, but to know you as a person. But to be honest, I'm not sure I want to know you that way considering how you treated me during your time here."

"Yes, you are right Baron. I have been called an Ice Queen, a bitch, and many other names since I have gone to work for the Auditor's Office. We have to be careful because of what we do and to be honest, most people hate us without knowing us. It's just…"

"It's just what Miss Marcos?"

"I've read up on you as I came to this world. Your Fleet Intelligence folder is interesting reading and before you say anything, we of the Auditor's Office have access to those files. I guess I expected much more from you is all."

"Much more? Miss Marcos, I have no idea what is in my file but you either misread it or someone has been posting information about me in it that is completely wrong. I do not chase women, I only try to be polite and considerate of them. Yes, I have had several lovers over the years and they came to me, I did not chase them. I too must be careful whom I allow in my bed because of who I am, my relationship to the Throne. Now with my wealth, it is even more so, it is a great burden to insure the person who enters my bed chambers is there for me, not for my money. Is there anything else, Miss Marcos?"

"Only that I wish I had met you before you discovered this world and its wealth. Good day Baron."

He noticed she had a tear slowly forming in her eyes as she turned away from him. He watched her board her shuttle and lift back to her transport. Carlos stood watching the shuttle disappear into the clouds thinking about what she had said about meeting him before he came here.

Carlos walked into his office and contact his personal ship and told them not to allow the Auditor's transport to boost out of orbit until he said so. Five minutes later he received an acknowledgement from the transport ship Captain of his orders.

He sat in his office, looking out towards the mountains to the north, thinking about what she has said about wishing she had met him before he had discovered his wealth. It was over an hour after he had restricted the transport from leaving that he received a message from the transport. Miss Marcos wanted to know why they were not being allowed to boost out of orbit.

Carlos sent a message back to the transport that Miss Marcos was to be at his estate in four hours for dinner, manner of dress was her option. They could discuss when he would allow them leave Marta's World at that time.

When she arrived, she was dressed as she had always dressed in a loose fitting jump suit. As before, Carlos met her at the gate and the look she carried this evening was not one of defiance as before, but one of distrust, even caution concerning the events which were to take place this night.

She stopped short of Carlos.

"Baron Gannaway, why are you doing this?"

"Miss Marcos, I am not looking for a playmate this evening, but I am looking for intelligent conversation. Granted it would have been better if I had not stopped you from boosting out of orbit, but you said you wished that you had met me before I discovered this world. So I give you a choice. Come, and hopefully enjoy a pleasant dinner with me as my guest, or get back on that shuttle and leave, return to Hanover this night. I place no further restrictions on your travel, nor do I expect anything except your company at my table and nowhere else."

She looked at him for a moment before accepting his offered arm and they walked together to his home. He took her directly to the dining room where the table was sat with heated, covered dishes awaiting them. Carlos assisted her in sitting then asked if wine was alright with her tonight or did she prefer a fruit drink. She accepted the wine and after tasting it, approved the flavor and her poured her half a glass, then began to uncover the dishes.

"Baron, the food smells delicious. You have a wonderful cook from the fragrance."

"Miss Marcos, I do not have a cook, or maid. Well, except for two ladies, wives of my employees who come once a week to clean the house. I cook, do my own dishes, my own laundry. We are alone in this house, but if that makes you nervous, I can call in a Lancer to insure that I will not take advantage of this situation with you."

"No Baron, this is fine."

"Miss Marcos, must you consistently refer to me as Baron? Especially here at my table as we get to know each other?"

"No Carlos, but only if you refer to me as Deyanna."

Carlos smiled as he took his own seat.

Since she had read his Intelligence file and seen other reports about him, she already had to decent level of knowledge about his background, so Carlos prodded her to speak about herself so he would know about her.

Deyanna was born on Altair to a father that was a chemist and her mother was a biologist. She had always been good with numbers, and was even recruited into the Auditor's Office while she was still in the university. She admitted she had a couple of lovers while in the university, but except for one long term relationship once she started to work at the Office, as she referred to the Auditor's Office, her social life was nonexistent. And that relationship ended over a year before she was handed this assignment to audit him.

Carlos tried to keep the conversation light and avoided asking her what she meant when she said she wished they had met earlier. She did compliment on his ability to cook, and asked what manner of meat the filet was he had prepared. The meal was light in substance but heavy on flavor as he was unsure how her tastes ran.

The meal ended with a fruit parfait and a final glass of wine. He escorted her out to her shuttle where she asked him another question.

"Here I had a wonderful meal, but what of my shuttle crew?"

"Deyanna, as soon as we entered my house, the Lancers took your shuttle crew to their mess facility and insured they were fed. The Lancers on average eat better than I normally do, so they were well taken care of. After all, we did spend a lot of time talking between bites and after dessert."

"Yes we did. Thank you for a pleasant evening."

She leaned over and kissed him on the cheek before boarding the shuttle.

"Pleasant dreams." He called out to her before she disappeared inside the shuttle.

Carlos walked back to his house and began to clean up from the dinner. She was hiding something but that was alright as he figured they would boost soon since he had made it clear before dinner he would not stop her again from leaving the planet.

It was a pleasant evening as far as he was concerned and once she loosened up, she seemed to be a pleasant individual. He understood her hesitation in being friendly when they first met since it was her job to either clear his books or hang him out to dry for failure to maintain proper accounting and properly pay his taxes.

He also had to laugh at himself as he did the dishes, thinking he could more than afford a cook and housekeeper, yet maintain his bachelor status doing all that himself except for the two ladies that cleaned the house for him.

Not My Fault!

Carlos had gone to the smaller continent to check on the drilling going on there for petroleum early the morning after the dinner. He had been informed that the transport had boosted from orbit within an hour after Deyanna returned to the ship. But as he made his landing approach with his personal shuttle to the pad behind his house, he saw another shuttle on the guest pad in front of the house.

When he exited his shuttle, Deyanna was standing near his back patio in the company of a Lancer waiting for him. She came to him as he was walking towards her.

"Baron Gannaway, what did you do after I left last night?"

It was easy to see she was not happy being back in his company.

"Miss Marcos, I have no idea what you are talking about. The only thing I did last night was clean up after dinner and go to bed. Would you care to explain what you are talking about?"

"We had barely boosted out of orbit when orders came for me to stay and audit the New World's, especially to look for items that will assist their advancement to modernization."

"Miss Marcos, Deyanna, this is news to me. The Marta Foundation has that well in hand. Maybe your superiors wish you to audit the Foundation to insure no graft is present, but regardless, I had nothing to do with your return to these worlds."

"Carlos, my orders are to disembark here, on Marta's World, and my transport is to return to Hanover without me."

"How old are you Deyanna?"

"What does that have to do with my staying here.....oh."

"Please how old are you and is this your first assignment away from Hanover?"

"I'm twenty-five and no it isn't, but it is the first alone instead of being part of a team. Carlos are you thinking what I am thinking?"

"Deyanna, I refuse to answer that on grounds I think we both might be right. I left early this morning to inspect the drilling operations and have not had a chance to check my messages. Regardless, you have valid orders and I would not be much of a host if I did not try to make you comfortable. Go back to the ship and gather your things, you can stay in one of my guest rooms until other arrangements can be made for you."

"All of my things are on the shuttle."

"Alright, do you need any help getting them?"

"No, I can deal with my bags, but this is unreal."

"Deyanna, go get your bags so the shuttle can lift while I go check my messages."

When he checked his messages, he found one from Aunt Connie, not Princess Consuela or The Throne. In it his aunt mentioned that Deyanna Marcos is distantly connected to the Denoyelles family via a distant aunt who had married into the family. Connie went on to say she felt that he needed someone detached from the Marta Foundation to monitor the funds and insure they were getting value for their money.

Deyanna set her bags on the floor of the main room then found Carlos at his desk, reading the message and the look on his face frightened her. There was no doubt he was upset and she was afraid he would take it out on her. He looked up and saw her.

"Come here Deyanna and look at this message from my aunt."

Deyanna did as asked and read the message as she understood why Carlos was upset.

"Carlos, is your aunt, the Princess trying to play match maker, putting us together this way?"

"Deyanna, so it seems and she isn't even trying to hide the fact. Stay put as I reply to her message."

Deyanna stood aside as he typed in the reply to his aunt.

"My Dear Aunt Consuela. Keep your nose out of my private life as this is a weak attempt to put myself together with Miss Marcos. This is one of the very reasons I left what passed for civilization because it seemed at every turn, someone was trying to mate me to another. Miss Marcos is a lovely female and pleasant company once she gets past her employment, but even though there is some animal attraction between us, I have no intention of jumping into a marriage with her, or even jumping into bed. So please my sweet Aunt Consuela, stay the hell out of my private life!"

Deyanna grabbed his hand before he could transmit the message.

"Carlos, do you really think you should send that message. I know you are angry, but your aunt is the Princess."

"Deyanna, this is one of her less subtle attempts to get me married off. I've already had this discussion with my parents, but apparently Her Royal Pain In The Ass Highness did not get the word. Don't get me wrong, I do love my aunt, but this is the last straw. As I said before, I left, ran away because of this kind of nonsense."

Carlos hit the transmit button, then stood up and looked at Deyanna.

"Another time or place I would have enjoyed knowing you in every possible way, but right now I am too upset to even consider the possibility. Take any room you wish in the house for your own."

He stepped around her and walked out of the office. A few minutes later as she was placing her bags in the room farthest from his, she heard the shuttle lift.

It would be a week before he returned to his estate.

Also during that week, Deyanna did the best she could as she waited for further orders. Since she was not tied into the communications system, she could not receive any messages via her pad, but once people realized that Carlos was not responding to messages, or that Deyanna was not responding, the Lancers were contacted and they brought Deyanna into their system.

Deyanna received messages from Aunt Consuela and Carlos's parents wanting to know what was going on with Carlos. Why he was not answering his messages to which she only replied he had left the estate and she had no idea where he had gone. The Lancers had only responded with those requests with he was still on the planet and was under their watchful eye, but did not respond telling them what he was doing, except that it appeared he was surveying the planet.

The truth was the Lancers had become very close to Carlos and he asked them to maintain as much silence as possible without getting themselves into trouble with the Throne. What Carlos had done was land on the second continent, took his survival pack and had walked into the deep forest and just sat there thinking, away from the electronic world.

Carlos never went to his message center to check on messages, but had contacted his Chiefs from the shuttle to keep things moving as he was going to the New World and check on a few things. When he landed at his estate, Deyanna told him of the messages which he said he knew about them as the Lancers had already informed him about them. He told her to answer them any way she felt was proper, otherwise not to bother him with them.

Carlos left the house an hour later with two Fleet duffle bags, boarded his shuttle and lifted to the Destroyer assigned to him, leaving Deyanna behind. Three days later he stepped off the shuttle onto the New World, and was taken to the former home of Moshe which he had renovated for his personal use. During the night, Carlos avoided the Lancers guarding this home and made it to the ship belonging to Ralph Childress which was still sitting on the pad after a complete overhaul. He lifted from New World and as soon as he cleared the planet, he went to full boost, heading deeper into unknown space.

He had nearly a twelve hour lead on the prospect of pursuit by the Fleet when it was discovered he had managed to avoid detection as he fled civilization to parts unknown.

The later conversation between Carlos's parents and his aunt was best left unheard outside of the family as his father ripped into his elder sister for setting Carlos up for marriage. He told her that unless it was business of the Throne, to keep her nose out of Carlos's business, and he was not polite is telling her. The last image of his sister that Lucen Gannaway saw was of tears flowing down her cheeks.

Baron Lucen Gannaway then contacted the Wainwright, Carlos's transport Destroyer and ordered them back to Marta's World and to pick up Deyanna Marcos and to bring her to Hollis to meet with him and Carlos's mother.

Four days later, Deyanna was on board the Wainwright in Carlos's personal cabin, and boosting for Hollis and Federation space.

Into the Unknown

There was now doubt in Carlos's mind he was a coward. He was running away from the responsibilities of his family and the prospect of having someone to grow old with. Deyanna Marcos was intelligent as she was lovely, and there was no doubt in his mind he would love to see her lavender body laid across his bed after a night of passion.

Deyanna also had admitted over dinner that she felt some attraction to him which was the reason why she asked how come he had not made a pass at her during the audit.

Two people isolated on a world where the only other people on it were either working for Carlos or protecting him from harm. But protecting him from what harm? Unless the Lancers were holding back on him any information concerning his welfare, then they were just standing around doing nothing.

As the stars rushed by his observation window, he thought about his escape on the New World. Lancers are not known for being lazy and inattentive. Did they suspect he was running and understood how he was feeling and just let him go? No, that could not be it because their own pride would be at stake if that was the case. The years of being around Lancers and Marines, going into the woods with them when he was young may have paid off for him.

During the trip from Marta's World to the New World, he had sent a message to the Marta Foundation Office on New World to stock this ship with supplies for a years plus journey as Ralph Childress was returning to collect his property. But Ralph Childress was on Bellus, going through treatments for several malady's he had contracted during his stay in the cage on New World.

Carlos just let the engines burn until he felt he had more than enough ballistic trajectory to take him far away from his family. Take him away so he could think in the cold darkness of space.

What Carlos did not know was that within hours of the discovery of him missing along with the ship, four Scout ships departed the Gannaway region to intersect with his ballistic path and to see if they could catch up with him before he radically changed course. Eighteen hours later they fell in behind Carlos with their ships cloaked so he would not see them following behind. Their orders were to follow and observe but only interfere with his journey if he was in danger.

Three months after Deyanna left Marta's World, she walked into the home of Lucen and Patrina Gannaway, Carlos's parents to find that Princess Consuela was also present, sitting off to the side, away from the others. Deyanna was uncertain what to do until the Princess spoke.

"Miss Marcos, today I am only Carlos's aunt, not the Princess and certainly not the Throne. I am only here to attempt to make amends for my actions concerning my nephew, Carlos. Please attend to my brother Lucen and his wife, Patrina."

"Miss Marcos, please sit and talk with us." Lucen offered.

"Baron Gannaway, I do not understand what has been happening. Can't I just go back to Hanover and do the job the Federation is paying me for?"

"Yes, I'm certain it can be arranged for you to return to Hanover, but first I wish to ask you a couple of questions. And I expect an honest answer. Do not think you can temper your answer just to please us as we have great respect for the truth, even if it is painful in reception. Understand?"

"Yes Baron, I understand."

"Do you have any feelings for our son besides sexual desire?"

"Baron, we hardly know each other. He is a kind and giving individual from all of my observation of him. If you are asking if I am in love with him, no. But if you are asking if I thought love could develop between us, then that is possible with any two people is it not?"

Patrina Gannaway laughed at Deyanna's response.

"Deyanna, forgive me for laughing but I can remember having the same thoughts when I met Lucen. Even as I thought I wanted him to make love to me, I assaulted his character and insulted him, trying to see if what I knew about him was reality or myth. Why he ever decided to finally take me to dinner so we could get to know one another still baffles both of us, but here we are now, lovers and parents to our children."

"Baroness, I have no answer for your comments."

"There are none expected. But let me ask you this. If given a chance, would you consider learning more about Carlos, learn if you are capable of loving him?"

Deyanna sat for a long time pondering the question.

"Baroness, that is an unfair question. What if I say yes and he rejects me. Then I am full of heartache to only watch him walk away from me. Before he left, he told me he was tired of the life he had to live as a member of this family. Tired of his family trying to marry him off. So if this is part of that same game, then I'll have no part of it, even if the Throne directs me to play the game. No Madam, I will not be a part of this."

Lucen smiled as Deyanna spoke then when he spoke it was not to her but to his sister.

"You were right Connie, she would make the perfect addition to the family, but you heard her, she'll not play the game and I for one applaud her for it."

"What is going on here?" Deyanna asked.

141

"Miss Marcos, you are free to go. The Captain of the Wainwright has been instructed to take you to Hanover or any other location you desire to go. Once there he will return to Marta's World and await for Baron Carlos to return to his estate." Princess Consuela advised Deyanna.

"No, I'm not going anywhere until I know what is happening here!"

"Consuela, Patrina once told Father where to stick it and it seems Deyanna just did the same with you. Now before Her Royal Highness climbs back upon her horse, Deyanna let me explain a few things to you."

He paused looking at Deyanna.

"Carlos is often the petulant child in that he runs away from adversity. But the interesting thing is he is not running because he is scare although if you ask him he would say otherwise, but he does this to be able to think without any outside influences. My sister put him in a position he does not believe he is ready for after the loss of someone he cared a lot for, someone he was considering marrying. But that was several years ago and I agree that he should be past that now."

Deyanna just nodded her understanding.

"Now regardless how this has all happened, it has happened and for one, I do not want you uncomfortable with your situation in regards to Carlos. I would much rather see you set up house in New Brunswick which is about as far away as you can get from Carlos then enter into a relationship you neither desire or feel comfortable with. Am I clear on this Miss Marcos?"

"Yes, Baron you are clear and thank you for the curtesy."

Lucen stood and offered his hand to Deyanna who also stood and took his hand.

"Miss Marcos, may the Saints watch over you in your travels. There is nothing holding you here now."

"Thank you Baron, Baroness, Your Highness."

She left the house and entered the aircar which brought her to this place for her ride back to her shuttle and the Destroyer Wainwright. What she didn't see was what happened once she had left the Baron's home.

"Connie I still think what you did was despicable, but what do you want to bet she goes back to Marta's World?"

"I'm not taking that bet Lucen but time is running out, and Carlos is our best choice here."

"Connie, he doesn't need to be married."

"No, but it will provide stability, an anchor."

"How much longer?"

"Two years at best."

"Damn it all"

Carlos just let the ship take him where ever it was going with any sense of direction in space. He knew the on-board computer would take him back to the New World if he told it too, but he wasn't ready yet.

On Hollis, Baron Lucen Gannaway smiled at the message from the Wainwright that they were heading back to Marta's World with Miss Marcos.

Right About Here

Carlos had been on this course for almost six months when the ship's sensors picked up a Class M planet just to port of his path. He adjusted course and programmed an orbit into the computer and just sat back to watch the planet grow in his window.

As the ship entered orbit, Carlos almost panicked as the sensors reported massive structures on the only continent on the planet, then picked up what the sensors said were space craft on the surface. Carlos was concerned he had stumbled upon a raider or slaver base on this world.

Carlos put more power into the sensors and the reading coming back showed the vessels on the surface were barely reading any power, which to him, meant they were abandoned. He was recording every pass over the planet, gathering every bit of data he could as he shifted a portion of his sensors off into space to insure he was alone out here.

He had the ships computer run the location of this world in relationship to Gannaway twice to make sure he had it right, then sent it too his pad. He then unpacked his personal crystal, linked the pad to it and sent it to his parents along with the early sensor readings.

After seven orbits of this world, Carlos became edgy, thinking he was being watched and programmed the ballistic computer to take him back to Gannaway at best possible speed. As the ship came around the planet and registered its position against Gannaway's, the engines went to automatic boost for home. What he did not see was two Scout ships scrambling to get out of his way as they stood off observing his orbits of this newly discovered worlds.

As Carlos was boosting towards home, the Scouts were ordered to leave two ships at the new world to observe it until relieved by a Fleet which would soon be heading to the planet and the other two Scouts to escort Carlos home.

Two months into his return trip, Carlos was passed by an eight vessel Fleet heading to the world he had discovered. He received a message on the Federation's Emergency Frequency stating; "Well Done, Baron."

Carlos computed the speed of the Federation ships based upon distance and knew they were well past Gannaway when they were sent to the world he had discovered. Class M planets were not as rare as people thought, but finding one with the mineral riches such as Marta's World or with ruins as the one he had discovered were indeed rare.

He just sat back and watched the stars once more pass by as he considered his situation. Carlos had heard his crystal beep a notification four times since he sent the report, but had yet to respond to it. He knew he was delaying the inevitable by not answering the calls, but this was his life, not theirs to run.

A month out, he recomputed his course to take him to the New World's where he had stolen this ship. He was going to wait until he was at his home if possible to face his parents and possibly his aunt.

Upon arrival at the New World's home world, the ships updated navigation system landed the ship with ease and without Carlos having to override the system. His bags were packed and when he stepped off the ship, he saw his shuttle sitting a few meters away having landed after he did. He just walked from one ship to another and took a seat.

No one spoke to him on the shuttle or on the Wainwright once he was aboard the Destroyer. He walked unescorted to his quarters and upon entering found he was not alone.

We Meet Again

When Carlos entered his stateroom aboard the Wainwright he found Deyanna Marcos sitting on his bed. He dropped his bags at the door, closed it and started towards her as she stood up.

"No Carlos, come no closer. I have been like a nun in a convent living in your home on Marta's World since you left. Your father gave me access to the personal journals of your ancestors and I have spent the past ten months reading them. I understand now what you have been feeling, been going through deep inside and I will not say I am sorry for you, on how you were raised and how you have to present yourself to the rest of the universe, but I believe you can be yourself and still honor your ancestors."

She paused for a moment.

"I have a room down the corridor from here that I am going to sleep in while aboard this ship with you. I still have the room you offered me in your home which I will sleep in back on Marta's World. You are forbidden from entering either room until we have time to learn about each other, to learn if it is possible that we can be more than acquaintances or even lovers. We, both of us, have been given this one chance and we should take advantage of it."

Carlos rubbed his unshaven face as he looked at her.

"Alright Deyanna, we'll take this one chance. To be honest I figured I'd never see you again."

"Is that what you wanted Carlos. To leave and return to find I had left, returned to Hanover?"

"I left because I was afraid to fall in love with you then to have you leave me because there was no love to return."

"Then we are both victims of the fear of failure. Failure to make the other fall in love with us. We may ultimately learn to hate each other as we live in separate rooms during this test period."

"Deyanna, I'm tired of running. Tired of being afraid to find myself one day old and alone. I'm game here if you are."

Deyanna walked to Carlos, wrapped her arms around his neck and kissed him as if he was a long lost lover returning from a long journey. She broke the kiss, and released him.

"That is as good as it gets for now, and I have to admit, I wanted to do that long before you took off into the unknown."

She left him standing in his room with a smile on his face.

The next morning, ship time, Carlos stepped out of his stateroom to find two Marines standing on either side of his door. He stepped out into the corridor and noticed two more Marines standing three compartments down from his. He looked at the Marine Sergeant standing at Parade Rest.

"Sergeant, care to explain what you are doing at my quarters?"

"Sir, the General ordered that your quarters will be guarded at all times while aboard the ship and a Marine will escort you during any movement aboard the ship, Sir."

"The General meaning my father, am I correct?"

"Yes, Sir."

Carlos looked back down the corridor.

"I suppose that is Miss Marcos's quarters?"

"Yes, Sir."

"When did the General order this protection?"

"Overnight Sir."

"Yes, well, I guess we cannot disobey the General, even if he is retired from service."

"With all due respect Baron, there is not a Marine alive that would disobey the General. We might fudge orders from Her Highness, but never the General's, Sir."

Carlos chuckled.

"Sergeant, I have argued with the General several times. Winning is hard, and losing is painful. But let me warn you, it's not the General or the Princess you need to concern yourself with, it's the Baroness. Who do you think keeps the General in line?"

The Sergeant smiled.

"Yes Sir, so noted Sir. There has been rumors about the Baroness, but you are the first to confirm them Sir."

"Carry On Sergeant."

Carlos walked down to Deyanna's quarters and pressed the call button by the door.

"Who is it?" Came her voice through the intercom.

"Carlos."

"Come on in, the door is open."

Carlos stepped in and immediately closed the door behind him. Deyanna was beside her bed wearing matching black thin panties and nearly a bra as she was getting dressed. She continued to dress as she spoke to him.

"What are you drooling at sailor?"

"Damn woman, seeing you like that gives a man impure thoughts."

"Well keep those thoughts to yourself for now. If we act on them too soon, it could mess everything up between us."

"Fair enough, but the next time I am at your door and you are still dressing, let me know and I will wait in the corridor until you are dressed."

"Sorry, you're right, I should have been more considerate." She picked up her blouse and slipped it on, then her skirt. "What brings you to my room this morning?"

"I came to take you to the Mess for something to eat as part of our getting to know each other project."

He then told her about the Marines outside her door, which was why he had closed it when he saw her manner of undress. She never commented on that aspect of his returning as they went to break their fast.

The trip back to Marta's World was spent talking, often as they toured the Destroyer with a pair of Marines close behind. If they were in his stateroom, Carlos left the door open so no one would talk about their personal conduct aboard ship which Deyanna thought was somewhat cute in context.

When she brought up the pinging noise his crystal would make from time to time, he only commented when he got home, then he would deal with whomever keeps trying to contact him.

Upon arrival at his estate, Carlos went directly to his office with the intention of finally facing those trying to contact him. But instead he became distracted by the stack of folders on his desk. The folders containing the production reports from the various operations on the planet he put aside for later.

Next was a message that the inhabitants of the New World's had finally determined a name for their home world and race. From the date of the message forward, their home world would be known as Panterra, as they were now Panterrians.

As he was going over the information on his desk, Deyanna sat in a chair off to the side, just waiting and watching him work.

When his crystal pinged, he uncased it to answer the contact, which at that point she stood up to leave. He waved her back to her seat, then opened the connection to find his father on the other end.

"Yes, Father?"

"Carlos, is there a reason you have been avoiding answering calls from myself and your aunt?"

"Yes Sir, there is. I'm no longer twelve and dependent upon the family. Granted I am grateful for all of the family assistance in setting up my operations here and the Foundation, but I'm my own man now and intend to live my life as such."

Baron Lucen leaned back from his crystal and then smiled.

"I've always said you were more like your mother than me. Alright Carlos, now what?"

"Well Father, you contacted me so is there something I need to know or is this purely a social call?"

"The ruins on the world you found during your trip, appear to be a couple centuries old. Research teams are headed there now to take them apart, brick by brick to see if they can discover their origin. Vids of some of the visible writings looks similar to the ones found by your ancestor, Prince Alexander. The paperwork showing you as the discoverer of that world has been processed and until the Federation releases the planet for settlement, all you get is credit at this time."

"Thank you Father, but I want nothing from it." Carlos looked over at Deyanna. "I have everything I want or need right here."

"Regardless, the world is yours unless they uncover hidden inhabitants on it. Now I have to ask. What is the status of you and Miss Marcos?"

"Why don't you ask her that Father? She's sitting to my right, out of the way and listening to this conversation."

"No, I'm asking you."

"Father, at the moment our relationship is hands off, purely plutonic in nature. When that might change is up to Miss Marcos and when it does happen, we are not going to run blabbing to you and mother."

His father laughed and leaned forward, breaking the connection between them. Carlos looked over at Deyanna who once again stood.

"Well, that was embarrassing." She said to him.

"What did I say wrong?"

Deyanna just shook her head and left the room with Carlos wondering what he had said that was so wrong. Carlos went back to reading the files on his desk and lost track of time in doing so. Deyanna returned to his office with a fruit salad and told him to eat as it was past time for the mid-day meal.

Carlos ate as he read and once the salad was gone, he turned around and found the salad dish was missing, gone from his desk. He had been so consumed with the production reports, he never noticed she had taken the dish from the desk.

The evening meal was a repeat of the mid-day meal except the salad had thin slices of spiced meat mixed with the vegetables. This time the dish stayed on his desk until she broke his concentration by rubbing his neck.

"Carlos, it is late and you should be in bed, resting. Those reports will be there tomorrow and they are only the reports of what was accomplished while you were gone. Please, get up and go to bed. Good night Carlos."

She leaned over and kissed him on the cheek, then picked up the dish and left his office. Carlos knew she was right and just left the open folder on his desk and went to his room. He was nearly undressed, thinking a shower before bed would be nice when the door to his room opened and Deyanna stepped in wearing a robe.

"Carlos, today you told your father you had everything you needed or wanted already on this world and you were looking directly at me when you said it. Did you mean it, what you said?"

"Yes Deyanna, I meant it and I meant it as I looked at you, because I believe you are what I need in my life."

Deyanna opened her robe to expose her nude body and as she walked to him, she let the robe fall to the floor.

It was two days before Carlos returned to his office to finished with the files as they only left his bedroom to eat. Four days later, Carlos took Deyanna up to the Wainwright and had the ship's Captain marry them.

Carlos did not notify his parents, but let them discover the marriage when the Captain posted the marriage to Fleet records.

Marta's Return

Carlos and Deyanna had been married for nearly a year when Marta returned to the planet with her daughter, Tikka in tow. He met her at the shuttle pad with Deyanna at his side. It was quickly noticed that the scars on her face had been removed and she walked with her head held high as she walked to him, holding Tikka's hand as they stopped about a meter from Carlos.

"Baron Carlos Gannaway, this is my daughter, Tikka. Tikka, this gentleman is the Baron Carlos Gannaway, and the lady with him is his wife, the Baroness Deyanna Gannaway."

Carlos immediately noticed she had lost the lisp she once had and now had an accent, making her words crisp and easy to understand. Tikka gave a small curtesy as she looked at the adults she had been introduced too.

Carlos went to one knee and looked at Tikka.

"My Lady Tikka, it is an honor to meet you."

"Thank you Sir. Mother tells me you are responsible for our medical treatments and education."

"Yes Tikka, I am. Was that wrong of me?"

"Oh no Sir. Mother tells me that she could not speak until you sent her to Altair and that she had been badly injured, but the Altairians repaired her injuries. Again thank you Sir."

Carlos smiled then stood back up to look at Marta.

"Marta, it is very good to see you again. What are your plans now?"

"Lord Carlos, I have no plans at the moment, but I understand you have no servants in your home. I owe you so much that I can never repay and before you comment otherwise, it is I who will determine who owes whom for the past. If you will allow me, I would take employment in your house as cook and maid. When the Baroness is with child, she will need someone to help her, and I have increased my knowledge of preparing meals."

"But Marta, I been advised of your education on Altair and you are more than qualified to return to Panterra and teach. Would that not be a better use of your education and time?"

"Lord Carlos, I want nothing to do with my home world except travel with you from time to time to show Tikka where I was born. But there are memories there I do not wish to revisit."

Before Carlos could answer, Deyanna spoke up.

"Lady Marta, we accept your offer and will insure that you are reimbursed properly, and that Miss Tikka receives a proper education with the other children of the workers here on this world."

"Thank you My Lady."

After Marta had settled her and Tikka into one of the guest rooms of the house, one of the female Lancers took Tikka to the play ground for the worker's children, and introduced her to the children playing there. It was during this time that Carlos talked in private with Marta about events after she left him to return to bond with Moshe.

"Lord Carlos, I knew you did not want me to leave with Moshe and I honestly did not want to go to him, but again, it was a matter of honor. Except he had no honor. He raped me as soon as we were in transit without going through the bonding ceremony. He kept me in his quarters and raped me as often as he could, always telling me that all I was good for, to accept him and his seed to produce him sons."

She took a sip of fruit juice before continuing.

"He made a mock showing of bonding with me once back on Panterra only to satisfy custom but he never took me gently, always harsh, forcefully and without pleasure. When I fought him, he had one of his men hold me as he tore out my claws, then when I covered myself with my tail, he cut it off, all the time laughing, telling me that I was going to give him sons even if I did not want too. As I think back on those horrible days, I think he was insane. But one time as he raped me, he told me that Lord Carlos would never have me once he was done with me."

"Marta, I don't know what to say except I am so very sorry for what happened to you."

"When it was known I was with Tikka, he gave me some relief, but caught me telling the other wives about my time with you and the kindness you and the other humans had shown me. He ordered me to be quiet and when I refused, he cut my tongue out, once more laughing that I was unfit for even him but he still raped me. One of the wives gave me the root to kill the pain and made me how you found me. He still raped me when he felt like it and all I could do at that point was to just be still and let it happen. The root numbed the pain and my mind as I suffered at his hands. It was he that stuck me in that room to hide me from guests and his men who came from time to time, hid me so others would not see his crimes against me."

No one spoke as Marta once again drank from her glass.

"Carlos, I don't even know when he cut my mane I was so numbed by the root. I just remember being taken outside from time to time by one of the wives and his assault on my body. I do not even remember when he clawed at my face and other parts of my body, scaring me so no one would ever have me but him. He was insane with the thought of you having me or me wanting you, and he was crazy with the thought of his own cowardice in facing you, so he took it out on me."

"Marta that was my greatest fear in that he would hurt you because of me."

"Carlos, as I sit here now, with the knowledge I have gained, I see now that the concept of honor is a powerful thing, but my former world took it to an extreme, one I was taught. If I knew then what I know now, I would not have left with him, would not have allowed myself to be place in a position to be raped and abused."

"But Carlos, I do remember that day you had me liberated from his grasp. I remember how you defeated him. My senses were not so dulled that I did not see what was happening around me. I just played the part so no one would inflict further pain on me. Carlos, your honor in defending me that day was false as we both know, but your anger for what had been done to me. It may have been your family honor and the Principals that prevented you from allowing me to leave this world, but it was your anger that you could not prevent what happened to me that set you upon the course you took when you faced Moshe. You allowed yourself to be injured as part of your own punishment in holding your honor above your concern for another because at the time, mine was a foreign culture, not protected under the Principals except to allow that culture to continue. Do not deny that I am in error, Carlos, because I have studied your family and the Principals and understand you more now than I could have ever before."

Marta looked at Deyanna who was sitting off to the side.

"Mistress, if Carlos had came to me, I would have allowed him to take me as a woman, but he understood that he couldn't, and I could not go to him. We could have been lovers but never in love as you are with him now and he with you. It was our honor that prevented that from happening. I have taken two lovers while I was receiving my education and they were both gentle and caring. But I no longer have any desire to take Carlos to my bed as any feelings for him is that I would have for an elder brother."

156

"Marta, I do not have those concerns about you and Carlos, but I am concerned about your life now that you are free to do what you wish."

"Thank you Mistress, but the most pleasant memories I have are here on this world named after me. It is here that I wish to stay, even if I must live alone with Tikka in another place. I wish to be of help to you and Carlos for all he has done for me once he rescued me, but I do not wish to be a burden on either of you."

"Marta, welcome to our small family, and there are no restrictions on you or Tikka." Carlos commented.

"Thank you My Lord Carlos."

An Unexpected Situation

Three weeks after Marta's return, Carlos was notified to be standing by to hear a speech from the Throne to the Federation's Universe. He was in his office with Deyanna by his side with his crystal connected to his parents, which was tied to Princess Consuela's so he could hear her speech as it was given.

They could see her as she began to speak and Carlos immediately knew something was wrong with her and as she spoke, her voice did not sound right.

"Citizens of the Federation, I come to you this day with unpleasant news. Years before I assumed the Throne, I contracted Krell's Disease while on a tour of the Eastern Rim with my husband and two children. As many are aware, Krell's Disease is treatable if caught early enough. Once our physicians became aware of the infection, they were vigorous in treating myself along with my family."

"It was thought that they had caught the disease in time and that I would continue with life as before, but it has returned inside of me, as it has my husband. It has not made another appearance in my children, but it is something which needs to be addressed."

"It is estimated that I have less than six months here on Keres before the disease advances far enough in me that I will not be able to attend to the business of the Federation. I have held lengthy discussions with the President of the Federation and key Ministers concerning the Throne and the individual who will occupy it once I am no longer able to sit upon it."

She coughed into a lace handkerchief, then continued.

"With the situation of my children also having Krell's Disease, it has been suggest they refrain from ascending the Throne. In talking to my son and daughter, they agree even though they have not had a relapse with the disease. In rejecting the

Throne, my children has placed the burden of the office in the lap of my brother, Baron General Lucen Gannaway."

Carlos felt a knot forming in his stomach.

"The Baron feels he is not capable of sitting on the Throne since his disability from his service to the Federation could be a handicap as he ages. This now places the line of succession to the Throne in the able hands of Baron Carlos Gannaway, Ambassador to the world, Panterra."

Carlos closed his eyes and prayed there was another way.

"The President of the Federation, with the approval of the Federation Council has stated that Baron Carlos Gannaway is more than acceptable as my successor. Granted, this is a deviation from the normal line of succession, but I hope the citizens of the Federation accept this deviation in succession and in a Federation wide vote, voice their approval of Baron Carlos Gannaway to take the Throne in order to maintain the heritage going back to Count Conrad Denoyelles in leading the Federation to even greater things in the future."

She paused as she took a sip of water before continuing.

"Carlos Gannaway, I know you can hear my voice, see my face as I speak these words. As with our ancestor, Princess Lujayn, you have been tested, but in a test of your own design and making and found to have passed that test. Your compassion for the people of Panterra is well known, and your generosity is equal to your compassion. Come to Keres and release me from my burden, and allow me to spend the rest of my time without the worries of the Throne on my body and soul."

The cry for Carlos to ascend the Throne was almost immediate across the Federation. And for the first time in his life, Carlos knew he could not run from this, run to find a place and time to think things through.

"Carlos?"

"I know Deyanna, I know. This is something I cannot run from even for a day. Time is short and we need to travel a long way. Please tell Marta she needs to pack her things for Keres, then we need to pack what we will need for the trip. I'm sorry Deyanna, but this is something I cannot turn my back on, not that I want the Throne, but because my family desires me on it."

"I know Carlos, I'll go tell Marta to get her and Tikka ready to travel. You better alert the Wainwright that we are boosting as soon as we can get aboard."

She gave him a short kiss then left to take care of his instructions. Carlos notified the Wainwright and even before he completed the call, the Captain in charge of the Lancers entered Carlos's office to inform him the entire detachment was on alert and standing by to turn his security over to a detachment of Marines that were dropping to protect him until he gets aboard the ship.

The Lancers would stay on the planet, insuring his estate was secure until he decided to maintain it as a getaway, or close it.

During the trip to Keres, Deyanna worked as his secretary, downloading volumes of information and insuring Carlos ate properly, exercised, and kept decent hours so he be fresh the next day cycle to start all over again.

In turn, he made sure she was protected from pregnancy as he wanted as much time alone with her before starting a family.

Taking The Throne

Krell's Disease attacks the muscles and nerves of the human body. It's origin is unknown and can hide within the body, undetected until it becomes active. It is also extremely rare, which is why there has been very little research done to protect against it.

It was thought the Princess Consuela had contracted the disease during an anthropological expedition she took part in during her days at the university, then transmitted it to her husband, and the children contracted it in the womb. But it was nearly three decades before it revealed itself and was first treated.

The actual ceremony in assuming the Throne was simple in that Princess Consuela was to hand over the sword once belonging to Count Conrad of Hanover, to Carlos, along with a scroll depicting his place in the line to the Throne. In the past this was done without fanfare in the private chambers of the reigning Prince or Princess.

But because of the unusual circumstances surrounding this change of the Throne, the ceremony was being broadcast across the Federation for all to see. Because of the time it took Carlos to travel from Marta's World to Keres and the Throne, Consuela had further succumbed to the disease and was physically unable to transfer the sword of Count Conrad to Carlos.

Consuela was in an air-chair in her royal robes with the straps holding her upright hidden by the robes. The sword and scroll were lying on a rest which did not touch her body even though it seemed they were on her lap. Before she had become too ill to even speak, Consuela had recorded her voice transferring the sword to Carlos.

At the time of transfer, the vid cameras did not show Consuela's face, but the view of Carlos, kneeling before Consuela as the recording was played and he reached forward to take the sword and scroll. Once in his hands, he stood and bowed to

Princess Consuela who then left the Throne room as Carlos walked to the Throne and laid the sword and scroll on it.

Carlos then walked over to a small, plain wooden table and sat down behind it in a simple, straight back chair. It had been immediately noticed that even his suit was a simple, businessman's attire instead of his Fleet uniform or other more regal apparel. He fingered the papers on the desk for a moment then moved them aside and looked directly at the center camera, unseen by the viewing audience, as he spoke to the universe.

"To all who can hear my voice, citizens and non-citizens alike. Today marks the end of an era and the beginning of another. Much has been written about those with the Denoyelles blood in our bodies, and the heritage resulting from the joining of the Princess Kaya of Bellus to Michael Denoyelles, my ancestors. Much of it is wrong, while too much of it is correct."

"Count Conrad Denoyelles understood that an individual is not truly free without the ability of self-rule. To be able to make his own decisions and petition those legally elected that determines the laws and regulations they must live under. It is why he set in place his Articles of Leadership, then stepped down from the Hanover Throne."

"Decades later, Princess Lujayn was taken to Hayuta to become their leader as the people demanded a ruler to watch over them and the Council of Elders that governed them. Her son, Prince Alexander stepped away from the Throne of Hayuta for the life of a forge master, basically hiding from the Hayutan people, forcing them to govern themselves."

"Princess Jilena had the Throne of Hayuta thrust upon her then later the Bellus Throne, along with the Protectorate of Keres and Zyra as the governing bodies of those worlds recognized that the Articles Count Conrad had set down had been corrupted and the rights of man, and woman, were being destroyed by the greed of a few."

"She then had the Hanover Throne forced upon her and with it, she used the military might of the worlds she had been given reign over to once more force out those who wanted to rule over the common individual for their own greed and power. Princess Jilena replaced the Articles of Leadership with the Principles of Leadership which Princess Lujayn had established during her rule of Hayuta."

"It is not the mission of the Throne to rule over the people of the Federation, but to insure that the Principles of Leadership are followed and that the basic rights of man, and woman are foremost in the minds of those who govern them."

"Behind me and to my right is the Federation Throne which is the symbol of leadership of the Federation and the known universe. I shall never sit upon that Throne as long as the Federation observes the Principals of Leadership and it's sub-articles as written by my ancestors. It is time, long past time for such a ruler to be a part of history, not making history."

"I shall not wear the robes of a Prince, but the suit of a Baron which Princess Consuela so knighted me as such. I shall always be available to be consulted with and advise the Federation Council in matters concerning the Principals of Leadership, but it is for them to govern, not I."

"To all who hear my voice attend to what I say to you this day. If I have to sit upon the Throne, to accept the title of Prince, then that means the people of the Federation have failed in their rights and duties to elect officials who were placed in office to see to the needs of their people and the Federation."

"The Fleet, with its Marines have pledged their loyalty to the Throne along with the Lancers. I also have the Home Fleets of nearly a dozen worlds to call upon. Do not make me use them to correct what you the people should control and correct."

"Now I call upon the scientists, the medical practitioners of the Federation to extend their research into diseases such as that which had fell the Princess Consuela. Submit your funding needs through your representatives on the Federation Council and be cautious in doing so. Graft will not be tolerated by my office, and I will unleash the Federation Auditing Office upon anyone or group thinking they can use Federation funds to enrich themselves. The rewards for finding a cure will more than compensate for your time and efforts."

"Next. The Federation exists in a bubble of less than four percent of the universe. Another planet has been discovered deep in space, away from the boundaries of the Federation which has ruins centuries old. It is time for the Federation to open it's boundaries through exploration. I am a prime example of the riches that are out there, awaiting to be discovered along with new races waiting to be joined with in peace. I hereby instruct the Fleet to prepare plans to expand our horizons, expand our borders for the future of mankind."

"I am Baron Carlos Gannaway. Heir to the Hanover Throne and the Federation. I have spoken and my word is my bond. May the Saints watch over each and ever individual hearing my voice and protect them."

The Reign

The Reign of Baron Carlos Gannaway was not without trouble, but he was able to refrain from taking the one step he had warned the Federation he would do if put to the test. All during his reign, the sword and scroll remained lying on the Throne were he had placed them the day he accepted them from Princess Consuela.

Deyanna continued to act as his secretary for the next thirty years as she gave birth to three sons, then Carlos asked the Fleet for Yeomen to assist him in his office.

Marta maintained the private quarters for decades with the help of two assistants and Tikka as she grew into a beautiful woman. Marta was courted by a Lancer Captain who had been detailed to command Carlos's security detachment and after two years of fending him off, she finally married him and gave him two sons.

Tikka went to the university on Zyra and studied biology, shifting to Altair for her doctorate degree. Her nearly coal black skin and fur coupled with her large bright blue eyes attracted all manner of suitors during those years, but she finally surrounded her heart to a Hayutan who was also on Zyra studying medicine. Their three children would go on to write new chapters in medicine as they became researchers into the various diseases found amongst the population of the Federation.

Carlos remained in the office of the Throne until his eightieth year when he and Deyanna retired to the estate on Marta's World where they first met. John Carlos, his eldest son ascended the Throne and like his father, refused to sit on it, but governed as he had seen his father do over the decades as his assistant.

The Federation had pushed its boundaries and technology during the years of Carlos's reign, expanding to nearly ten percent of the visual universe and developing engines for the Fleet that drove the ships faster, making transit times shorter. What took months turned into days of transit between worlds and systems across the Federation.

Carlos and his descendants took care in how they functioned as the Federation Throne. In a universe where distance was measured in Light Years, and the time to travel those distances had shrunk to weeks, Carlos wrote that he thought it was odd that the people within the Federation felt they needed royalty watching over them.

He wrote that to him, having a Throne to look upon, meant each citizen felt they were part of something bigger than themselves. And five generations after Baron Carlos Gannaway set the sword of Conrad Denoyelles on the Throne, it was still lying there, only to be moved when cleaned, and once when the Throne itself was replaced due to aging. But even then it was never picked up by the individual who held the title or was next in line to carry the title, but was moved by a member of the family, an individual with Denoyelles blood in their veins who was not in line to take the Throne.

And from the day that Carlos placed the sword on the Throne, there was a Lancer in full battle gear standing beside the Throne to insure no one except the person authorized to touch the sword, did just that.

Carlos and Deyanna are buried on Marta's World as is Marta and her husband. Marta was buried with the marker proclaiming her Lady Marta and is buried to the left, next to Carlos as Deyanna is buried to his right.

So ends the Saga of Carlos Gannaway, descendent of Conrad Denoyelles, and his attempt to avoid the Curse of the Family, often referred to as The Bellus Curse.

About The Author

Leon Michaels is the author of several novels and short stories that reflect his twenty-three years of military service.   Michaels enlisted in the Marine Corps in 1970 and has memberships in the Veterans of Foreign Wars, the American Legion, the Disabled American Veterans organizations, NRA, and Rotary International.   In 1971, he married his high school sweetheart, raised three daughters and has three grandsons. He calls Creek County, Oklahoma home.

Made in the USA
Columbia, SC
21 June 2018